"What if the kidnappers found him first?

"What if they hurt Jackson? What if they hurt the dogs?"

Scott put his arm around Lily. "The only way we're going to get out of this is to stay calm," he said.

She leaned into him, head on his shoulder. She was trembling slightly—was that from cold or fear, or something else? After a moment, she looked up at him. "When you were in the army, did you ever feel scared and hopeless?"

"I was afraid plenty of times," he said. "Anyone who says they aren't is lying. But I never let myself feel hopeless. I had too many other people depending on me for that."

She pressed her lips tightly together, then nodded. "Right. Jackson is depending on us. All the people who care about Jackson, too. And Hunter and Shelby are depending on us."

DANGER ZONE

CINDI MYERS

For Gini

Recycling programs for this product may not exist in your area.

ISBN-13: 978-1-335-69050-0

Danger Zone

For questions and comments about the quality of this book, please contact us at CustomerService@Harlequin.com.

Harlequin Enterprises ULC
22 Adelaide St. West, 41st Floor
Toronto, Ontario M5H 4E3, Canada
www.Harlequin.com

HarperCollins Publishers
Macken House, 39/40 Mayor Street Upper,
Dublin 1, D01 C9W8, Ireland
www.HarperCollins.com

Printed in Lithuania

Cindi Myers is the author of more than seventy-five novels. When she's not plotting new romance storylines, she enjoys skiing, gardening, cooking, crafting and daydreaming. A lover of small-town life, she lives with her husband and two spoiled dogs in the Colorado mountains.

Books by Cindi Myers

Harlequin Intrigue

K-9 Avalanche Rescue

Danger Zone

Eagle Mountain: Unsolved Mysteries

Canyon Killer
Wilderness Search
Peak Suspicion
High Country Escape

Eagle Mountain: Criminal History

Mile High Mystery
Colorado Kidnapping
Twin Jeopardy
Mountain Captive

Eagle Mountain: Critical Response

Deception at Dixon Pass
Pursuit at Panther Point
Killer on Kestrel Trail
Secrets of Silverpeak Mine

Visit the Author Profile page at Harlequin.com.

CAST OF CHARACTERS

Lily Alton—The newest member of SkyCrest Resort's avalanche dog team needs to prove she and her avalanche-dog-in-training, Shelby, are worthy to be part of the team.

Scott Linden—The ski patrol captain is a perfectionist who wants only the best for his team and has little patience for mistakes. His black Lab, Hunter, is his closest companion.

Jackson Endicott—The only child of a wealthy industrialist, Jackson is smart but sheltered, and a favorite with his former nanny, Lily.

Denton Endicott—The wealthy industrialist is devoted to his son and loyal to a fault when it comes to his friends.

Mike Swanson—Denton's right-hand man has worked for Denton for twenty-two years and knows all his secrets.

Preston Shipman—Denton's newest employee comes highly recommended, but Mike doesn't trust him.

Chapter One

"Look at the dog!"

"Oh my gosh, that's so cute!"

"I didn't know they allowed dogs on the ski runs."

"It's a ski patrol dog. Look at its red vest."

"Shelby! Come!"

Patroller Lily Alton skied to a stop a short distance from the tourists clustered around her Belgian Malinois, Shelby. A woman in a purple ski suit, two men in black pants and brightly colored jackets, and two little boys with shark fins on their ski helmets stood with a third man, who was eating a hot dog. The blonde dog with black muzzle was sitting at attention, focused on the hot dog. "Shelby, come!" Lily repeated.

Shelby jumped to all fours and whirled around. Upon spotting Lily she let out an excited bark and bounded across the snow toward her. The dog leaped into the air, slamming her front paws into Lily's chest. Lily bent backward, but managed to stay upright with her arms full of fifty pounds of squirming fur.

All around her, people began to laugh and applaud. Lily forced a smile and managed to set the dog down without injuring either of them. "What's its name?" A teenage girl skied up.

Lily winced as the girl's skis skimmed only a few inches from Shelby's paws. The dog was standing still now, looking from Shelby to the girl, plumed tail gently fanning the air.

"This is Shelby," Lily said. "She's one of seven avalanche search dogs here at SkyCrest Resort."

"Can I pet her?" One of the shark-fin-helmeted boys had joined them.

"You can. And thanks for asking."

Shelby's whole body wiggled with delight as the kids patted her. The dog sat, then slid to the ground, until she was writhing in the snow, both children rubbing her belly and giggling.

"Would you like a trading card?" Lily took two of the cards, which featured a color photo of Shelby on the front and details about her and SkyCrest's avalanche dog program on the back.

"Ooh, yes please," the girl said.

Lily handed out the cards. "You can collect the whole set," she said. "There's one for each of the avalanche dogs here at SkyCrest."

"Thanks!" the boy said.

Lily's radio crackled. "Alton. What's your twenty?" The crisp voice of Patrol Director Scott Linden cut through the static.

"I'm at the bottom of lift one," Lily replied.

"Well, get over here. We're all waiting on you."

"Ten-four." She clicked off the radio. "Shelby, come!" she called.

"Sounds like Scott is in his usual sunny mood," she told the dog when she pranced up to her.

Shelby wagged her tail in reply. Nothing the grumpy patrol director said seemed to affect the dog's sunny mood. If only Lily could adopt the same attitude.

She skied to patrol headquarters, left her skis in the rack at the bottom of the steps, then knocked snow off her boots as she stomped up the steps to the door.

A wave of warmth hit her as she stepped inside, followed by the smell of damp dog. Shelby trotted past her to greet Hunter and Darth, the two black Labs in the corner, then moved on to lick the goldendoodle, Farley, in the face. She ended her rounds at the feet of a tall blond man who frowned down at her. Shelby sat and looked up at the man expectantly.

The man, Ski Patrol Director Scott Linden, turned to Lily. "Why were you late, Alton?" he asked.

"A group of guests stopped me to ask questions," Lily said. Part of their job as ski patrollers was to interact with guests.

"The rest of patrol doesn't seem to have as much trouble getting to meetings on time as you do," Scott said.

"That's because we're not showstopper blonds," patroller Chase Sergeant said from his perch by the lockers. He held up his hands. "I was referring to Shelby, of course."

The dog in question had flopped onto her side, eyes closed. She was definitely a striking pup, her pale gold hair tipped with black, black socks, black upright ears and muzzle, and brown eyes that appeared to be lined with kohl.

Lily had light brown hair worn in a braid that hung from beneath her black ski helmet, an accessory that obscured most other features. So yeah, she was sure Shelby was definitely the one attracting all the attention as the pair traveled through the resort.

Scott stepped over Shelby to reach the middle of the patrol shack. In addition to the four dogs, the small space was crammed with seven patrollers, half a dozen pairs of skis, two toboggans, several backpacks, orange cones, rolls of snow fence, coils of yellow nylon rope, four shovels, a bundle of avalanche probes, two cardboard boxes overflowing with ski patrol T-shirts and an inflatable palm tree. "Sergeant and Donaldson, you're at Buttermilk Basin this morning," he began, reading from a clipboard. "Iverson and Castro, I want you at the Glades. Milk Run is closed to the public for race practice, so you'll want to keep an eye on that. Raz, I want you here at post one. Alton, you're with me at Top of the Mark."

Lily kept her expression neutral, even as she groaned inwardly. Shelby raised her head and met her gaze, always in tune with Lily's mood. Scott had an excellent reputation as a skilled patroller, but he had all the charm of a drill sergeant. At least his dog, Hunter, was a genuine sweetheart. The big black Lab stood now and stretched, front and back, then shook vigorously, his patrol harness jingling.

"Weather reports show a storm coming in after seven tonight." Scott continued reading from the clipboard. "They're calling for three to six inches overnight. Five a.m. start tomorrow."

This elicited groans from the gathered patrollers, though the early callout was routine on mornings after a snowstorm. They would spend hours on avalanche mitigation before the slopes could safely open to visitors.

"I'll have the ammo ready." Connor Donaldson, Farley's handler, was in charge of the explosives used for triggering controlled slides in inbound terrain.

"Alton."

Scott's voice had her sitting at attention. "Yes, sir?"

"We need to schedule Shelby's Level B certification," Scott said.

"Shelby already has her Level B certification," Lily said. "She received it last May."

"That was at Kingdom Mountain," Scott said.

"Yes." Lily had patrolled at Kingdom Mountain ski resort, west of here, for six years before the resort had shut down last spring, the last year with Shelby. They had transferred to SkyCrest, owned by the same corporation, this fall.

"I want you to recertify for SkyCrest," Scott said.

The room had fallen silent, everyone watching and listening to this exchange. "Shelby was certified by Wasatch Backcountry Rescue," Lily said. "She shouldn't need to be recertified."

"She's a new dog for us," Scott said. "I have no idea of her capabilities. I want her recertified. I'll set up the test in a few weeks and get back to you."

She stared, speechless. Part of her wanted to protest that he was only doing this because he hadn't wanted Lily and Shelby on his team to begin with. Management had announced the addition to patrol without consulting him and that, apparently, had irritated him. That didn't give him the right to take it out on her and her dog. But pointing this out wasn't going to win her any points with him. He was going to make her prove herself. She stood. "Fine," she said. Shelby rose also. "We'll be ready."

Her gaze locked to his for a brief moment. She was prepared to see a lot of emotions in his gaze—anger, disdain or even dismissal. What she didn't expect was the flicker of heat his direct stare sent through her. His hazel eyes weren't exactly friendly, but they were definitely—interested. Scott scrutinized her as if she was a puzzle he was trying to figure out. As if he *wanted* to figure her out.

She looked away as he dismissed everyone with his usual "be careful out there."

"I'll meet you up top," she mumbled, and hurried out of the lift shack, Shelby at her heels.

"Hey, Lily!" She paused and waited for Connor to catch up. Farley tackled Shelby and the two dogs rolled in the snow, then popped up and shook themselves, panting happily.

"Don't let Linden get to you," Connor said. With his shaggy ginger hair and clipped beard, he bore a passing resemblance to his dog. They definitely shared the same soulful brown eyes.

"What is his problem?" she asked. "He treats me like I'm a brand-new trainee who's never been on snow before."

Connor grimaced. "I think it's because you're the only dog handler he didn't personally select and train."

"So he knows more than Wasatch Backcountry Rescue and C-RAD?" Colorado Rapid Avalanche Deployment was the premier organization in Colorado for training and deploying avalanche dog teams for immediate response to avalanches anywhere in the state. Lily and Shelby had completed multiple classes with WBR and C-RAD.

Connor shrugged. "Scott founded the dog program here. It's his baby."

"That doesn't give him license to act like a jerk."

The man himself exited ski patrol headquarters in time to hear this announcement. His head snapped up, and he turned in Lily's direction. Now she'd done it. Well, she didn't care if he knew what she thought of him. She raised her chin, defiant, then planted a pole and skied away, Shelby bounding alongside.

As Lily approached the head of the line the liftie, Desi, signaled for the next group of skiers to wait and waved Lily and Shelby forward. The dog jumped into the lift chair, and Lily settled beside her. Shelby lay down, her head in Lily's lap, as the chair rose into the air. Lily buried her gloved fingers in the thick ruff of fur around the dog's neck. She reached the mid-mountain lift and rode it up to Top of the Mark, the highest lift-served terrain. This was the view touted in all the advertising for SkyCrest resort—snow-crowned peaks set against a turquoise sky. In addition to the lift-served runs accessed from "the mark," gates provided access to acres of hike-to terrain.

At the top of the lift, the chair slowed. Lily stood as her skis made contact with the ground and Shelby bounded gracefully off the chair and toward the ski patrol shack at the edge of the tree line a few yards away.

She was opening the door to the shack when Hunter trotted up behind her, followed quickly by Scott. Lily braced herself for a confrontation over her "jerk" remark, but he said nothing. "We'll leave the dogs here while we patrol," he said as he moved past her into the shack.

He was filling a water bowl for the dogs when she joined him inside. Both canines lapped noisily as soon as he set the bowl on the floor. "Come on, Hunter," he said, and opened the door to one of the kennels in the back corner of the hut.

Hunter obediently trotted into the kennel and curled up on the memory-foam pad there. Without Lily even asking, Shelby loaded into her own kennel. She was curled up, plumed tail over her nose, and asleep before Lily even closed the door.

Dogs secured, she followed Scott back out of the lift shack and stepped into her skis again while he secured the door. "Let's make a run down May Day," he said. "On the way up I got a complaint about kids hucking off the rocks there."

Hucking—or jumping—off the rocks above the ski runs presented a real hazard to both the jumpers and skiers below them. Patrol had roped off the area several times, but the ropes were easy enough to take down, and a group of local teens, supplemented by more daring visitors, regularly congregated in the area to test their mettle and the agility of the patrollers. So far, they had all escaped apprehension.

"Hey, Lily!" They had not skied far when a boy hailed her. She slid to a stop as nine-year-old Jackson Endicott skied up to her. Small for his age, with pale blue eyes, Jackson usually wore an earnest, slightly worried expression.

"Hi, Jackson," Lily said. "What are you up to?"

"I'm waiting on Dad." He looked up the slope, where a black-clad man had stopped to talk to a couple in matching red ski suits. "He's always stopping to talk to people." He looked back at Lily. "Where's Shelby?"

"She's taking a nap right now," Lily said. Aware of Scott waiting beside her, she gestured to him. "This is Scott Linden," she said. "Scott, this is Jackson Endicott."

"Nice to meet you, Jackson," Scott said. He even sounded friendly.

"Are you coming over tonight?" Jackson asked.

"I sure am. I'm looking forward to it."

"Cool. Oops, there goes Dad." Jackson jammed his poles in the snow as his dad sped by. "Gotta go." He rushed off, skis scraping as he worked up speed.

Lily and Scott set off behind him at a slower pace. "How do you know Jackson Endicott?" Scott asked.

"I was his nanny when he was a baby," she said. "Before he started school."

"Then I guess you've been inside their chalet."

"Yes." And their summer home in Maine and their winter retreat in Taos. "I still babysit for Jackson sometimes when his dad has to be away." Tonight was a client dinner. Though the Endicotts had a live-in housekeeper, Denny Endicott preferred to have Lily stay with Jackson. And since he paid twenty dollars an hour and all the food she could eat, she was happy to oblige. "How do you know the family?" she asked Scott.

"I don't know them, but I know *of* them. Denton Endicott is always in the news."

"Hmm." Lily didn't pay that much attention to the news.

"*The New York Times* did a profile of him a few months ago, about the proprietary navigational software he's developed. Apparently, it's a pretty lucrative business."

"I guess so."

"He might be a good person to approach about donating to the avy dog program," Scott said. "SkyCrest supports our avalanche dogs with some funds, but you know how expensive training and upkeep can be. We're always looking for private donors."

She gaped at him. "You want me to hit him up for money?"

"Why not? The program is something you're passionate about. Maybe he'd like to support it. You may not think about these things, but I have to." Not waiting for an answer, he sped up, quickly outdistancing her.

She was still processing the exchange when shouting ahead drew her attention. She skied around a curve and almost collided with a boy on a snowboard who zipped in front of her across the slope. A second boy braked to avoid hitting her and fell over backward in the snow. Lily hurried to help him up. "Are you all right?" she asked.

"That man grabbed my brother," he said.

Lily followed his gaze behind him, to where Scott stood, his hand clamped on the arm of a slightly older boy in a baggy blue jacket and wide-legged plaid pants. Lily looked back at the boy at her feet. "Were you hucking off the rocks?" she asked.

He stuck out his lower lip. "We made sure nobody was coming before we did it. We weren't hurting anyone."

"Come on, get up." She offered her hand to the boy. He hesitated, then took it, and she helped him to his feet. Then she pulled out a pair of scissors.

"You're not going to take my pass, are you?" the boy wailed.

"You can pick it up next week in the pass office," she said as she cut the nylon tie that attached his ski pass to his jacket. "That is, if this is your first offense. Second offense means you're done for the season."

"That's not fair!" the boy wailed. Up ahead, his brother was giving Scott grief. Lily skied up to join her boss.

"I got the brother's pass," she said.

"You people are going to hear from our dad," the older brother said. He was red-faced, frost forming on the nascent moustache above his thin upper lip.

"He's welcome to give me a call," Scott said. "I'll tell him how you were trespassing in closed terrain and endangering your own life and the lives of others." He pocketed the boy's pass. "Now ski down and go home."

They watched the two boys head down the run. Scott looked at the rocks above the run. "We need to go up there and restring the ropes."

"Easier to ski over from Daisy Chain," she said, naming the run that led above and behind them.

"Then let's do it."

They spent the next hour restringing the ropes, closing a narrow section of a run where the snow had melted off to expose rock, and redirecting skier traffic away from a lift that was temporarily closed due to a malfunction. Working with Scott wasn't as bad as Lily had feared. He didn't try to tell her how to do her job, and he was pleasant with the public. When two girls skied up to them, he stopped what he was doing and gave them his full attention. "Do you have any trading cards?" one, who looked to be about eight and wore a helmet with bunny ears, asked.

"Of the dogs," her friend with a bright purple helmet asked.

"Here you go." Scott offered cards featuring Hunter at the wheel of a snowmobile.

The girls squealed in delight, and squealed again when Lily passed over cards featuring Shelby's photo. "Where are the dogs?" purple helmet asked.

"They're resting up," Scott said. "Running around in the snow wears them out."

"Give them kisses for me," rabbit ears said. She hugged the cards to her chest. "I just love dogs."

"So do I," Scott said, his grin almost as big as the girls'.

Seeing him like this stunned Lily. "Who knew you were such a softy," she teased.

His smile faded. "Yeah, well, I only wish the rest of our job was as easy as interacting with kids." He checked his watch. "I've got a meeting I need to get to. You should check back in at the ski patrol hut."

"See you later," she said, and skied away. But she stopped at the top to look back at him—a tall, graceful figure gliding down the slope. Working with him this morning hadn't been so bad. He was good at his job, and good with people. If only he could see her as an ally, not an imposition.

Chapter Two

The rest of the day passed in a blur of activity, from marking hazards to tending to injured skiers. By four o'clock, all the lifts on the mountain shut down. Scott and Lily released the dogs from the kennels and closed the patrol shack for the night, switching off lights and the heater and locking the door. At four forty-five, they began their sweep of the runs, making sure everyone was cleared off the mountain before dark.

Lily and Shelby skied May Day, a long, wide run that ran for over a mile, all the way to the base area. This was her favorite time of day, when they had the snow all to themselves. Shelby, rested up and full of puppy energy, ran ahead of Lily, legs stretched out, puffs of snow flying up around her at each landing. Occasionally she stopped and rolled in the snow, the picture of pure joy.

Lily made long, sweeping turns, checking both sides of the run for any skiers or snowboarders who might have fallen or simply stopped to rest. Across the mountain, all the lift chairs hung empty and still, and lights began to bathe the ski village at the base in a golden glow, in anticipation of growing dusk.

Back at the base, she stowed her gear in her locker and fed Shelby her supper. A national pet food supplier donated a diet designed for active dogs to the ski patrol, so whenever they were working, meals were covered. While Shelby ate, Lily swapped her uniform for leggings and a tunic sweater. Then she grabbed her day pack and parka and headed for the shuttle stop. At her apartment, she transferred Shelby and her belongings to her car and set out again.

Fifteen minutes later, Lily was at the gate to the Endicotts' property. She lowered her car window and leaned out to press the intercom button. "Hi, it's Lily Alton," she said.

"Jackson's waiting for you," a gruff but not unfriendly voice said. Mike Swanson was Denny Endicott's right-hand man. The title on his business cards said senior analyst, but after Jackson's mother passed away when the boy was three, Mike had taken over as a kind of household manager/chief adviser to the busy executive. The two had apparently known each other since college. He was actually the person who had hired Lily to be Jackson's nanny six years ago.

The gate swung open, and Lily guided the Subaru up the winding drive and parked in a slot to the left of the garage. Shelby bounded out after Lily and ran to the open back door, where Mike waited. He was only a couple of inches taller than Lily's own five foot six, but he had the muscular build of a wrestler and the round face and bald head of a cherub. He bent to pet the dog, then looked up at Lily. "Denny said he's sorry he couldn't be here to meet you. He's entertaining some important clients."

"You aren't going with him?" she asked. Mike played a big role in the operation of Endicott Industries, also.

"I have a meeting of my own tonight."

The door from the kitchen to the rest of the house burst open and Jackson rushed in. "Shelby!" he cried, and dropped to his knees to embrace the dog.

Shelby, tail wagging exuberantly, licked Jackson's face while the boy giggled wildly.

"That's enough," Mike said. "Remember what happened last time you got Shelby too excited."

Behind his back, Lily made a face. The incident in question involved Shelby racing through the house with an expensive velvet throw in her mouth, flying out behind her like a flag while Jackson, shouting at full volume, raced after her. At least one imported vase—not to mention the throw—were casualties of the chase. Lily had spent most of the rest of the night terrified that she would spend the rest of her life paying back the cost of the damaged items. Fortunately, Denny had only laughed at Jackson's delight over the story. "Jackson says it wasn't your fault, and I believe him," Denny had said. "But try not to let it happen again."

Jackson stood. "No chases, I promise," he said. "What kind of pizza do you want, Lily?"

They had a tradition of ordering pizza whenever she babysat. "How about pepperoni?" she asked. It was Jackson's favorite. Hers too, as it happened.

Mike took a suit jacket from the back of a kitchen chair and slipped it on. "I'll leave you to it," he said. "Don't forget to set the alarm behind me."

She followed him to the back door and waited until he was in his car before she pressed the code to arm all the outside doors and windows. She guessed being a billionaire meant you had to be more careful about security, though she had always felt safe here in this beautiful, quiet home.

They ordered pizza, then headed for the den, where Jackson demolished her in a game of *Slime Rancher*.

The doorbell rang. "Pizza!" Jackson shouted.

"I'll get it." Lily hurried to the door, Shelby trailing behind. She checked the security peep, her hand already on the doorknob, but stopped short. The man on the other side of the door—tall, long-faced, prominent nose, close-cropped dark hair graying at the temples—was not the pizza delivery person. He wore dark slacks and a blazer and carried no delivery bag.

She pressed the intercom. "Can I help you?"

"It's Preston. I'm here to talk to Mike. Who are you?"

"I don't know a Preston."

"I'm a new hire for Endicott Industries. Look, here's my ID." He held up a card with the Endicott Industries logo and his photo. He was identified as *Preston Smith, Data Specialist.* She scrutinized it, then opened the door, leaving the chain on. "Mike isn't here," she said.

"Who are you?" he asked.

His demanding tone annoyed her. "I'm the babysitter."

Jackson moved in beside her. "Hello, Jackson," Preston said. "Would you please tell the babysitter I really do work for your dad?"

Jackson scowled. "He works for Dad," he said.

"Do you want to leave a message for Mike or Mr. Endicott?" Lily said.

"Why don't you let me in, and I'll write a note to leave."

She shook her head. "Not going to happen. I don't care if you are an employee, I don't know you and Mike isn't here."

He frowned and pocketed his ID card once more. "How long have you been babysitting for Mr. Endicott?" he asked.

"That's none of your business."

"Where did Mike go?"

"He said he had a meeting."

"Who was he meeting with?"

"I don't know. I think you'd better leave now." She didn't like this man or his attitude. She started to close the door but saw headlights sweep up the driveway. A battered compact car with a lighted sign for the pizza restaurant on the roof stopped in the driveway, behind a black pickup she assumed belonged to Preston Smith.

Smith turned to watch the young man with the pizza head up the driveway. He stepped to one side. "Good night," he said, and headed for his truck.

The pizza guy looked from the truck to her. "Something wrong?" he asked.

"Just stay here until he's gone," she said. She punched in the code to disarm the security system, then lifted the chain and opened the door all the way.

"Sure." He handed over the pizza, and they waited silently until the truck was out of sight.

"Thanks," she said.

"No problem."

She closed and locked the door, reset the alarm, then carried the pizza into the living room. Jackson sat on the floor in front of the coffee table. Shelby settled beside him, all her focus on the pizza. "I don't like that guy," Jackson said.

"Preston Smith?"

"Uh-huh."

Smith certainly hadn't impressed her. "Why don't you like him?" She opened the pizza, slid a slice onto a plate and passed it to Jackson.

"He's just—sneaky. Like, I caught him coming out of Dad's home office once when Dad wasn't home. He said he left some papers for Dad to look at but I think it was just an excuse to snoop." He took a bite of pizza. "Mike doesn't like him, either."

"Don't talk with your mouth full, please." Lily chose her own slice of pizza. "Why did your dad hire him, I wonder?"

Jackson swallowed and took a drink of Dr Pepper. "He's

supposed to be some genius or something. Anyway, I'm glad you didn't let him in."

"You should never let anyone in the house you don't know," she said. "Especially if your dad or Mike isn't here."

"Yeah. I know." He offered a piece of pizza crust to Shelby, who gobbled it up. "You could have threatened to sic Shelby on him."

Lily smiled at the dog, who was begging for more pizza. Shelby looked fierce, but she was really a cream puff. "Shelby isn't that kind of dog. She's bred to help people, not fight them."

"I guess so." Jackson reached for a second slice of pizza. "Are you working again tomorrow?" he asked.

"I am. Saturday is our busiest day."

"I wish I was going to be there," Jackson said. "But Dad said he won't get home until late, so I have to wait until next week."

"The snow may be even better next week," Lily said.

"Do you like your new job?" he asked.

"I do."

"That guy you were with today—he's your boss?"

"Yes. Scott is in charge of the avalanche dog program."

"He seemed nice."

Scott was...complicated. Like most people, she expected. Not the most charming man she had ever met. But everyone described him as "firm but fair." His insistence that Shelby be recertified for her Level B annoyed her, but he was clearly the kind of her person to cross all his t's and dot all his i's. And she had faith in Shelby. The dog was still young, but so smart and eager to please.

After pizza, they watched a movie. Jackson fell asleep before the end, and Lily woke him to put him to bed. Then she and Shelby relaxed on either end of the sofa, a rom-com she had selected from the Endicotts' endless streaming choices playing low on the television.

She must have dozed off. Shelby's low growl woke her, and she sat up as headlights played across the home's front windows. She waited, tensed, until she heard a key in the lock of the back door. It opened, then the beeping of the alarm keypad told her Denny was shutting off the alarm. She moved to the front hallway, smiling, intending to offer a cheerful greeting.

But the smile faded as she stared at Denton Endicott. The normally impeccably put-together businessman slumped against the wall, his navy-blue suit rumpled, one sleeve hanging loose, his thick graying hair in disarray. He glanced at her, and she gasped—one eye was swollen shut, the skin around it purple, his bottom lip puffy and bloody. "What happened?" she asked, rushing forward, hands outstretched.

But she stopped short of touching him. With effort, he straightened and waved her away. He stood over six feet, and though he had developed a paunch over the years, he still conveyed power. "It's nothing," he said.

He started to move past her, but she blocked his path. "You're hurt," she said. "Do you want me to call an ambulance?"

"No!" His voice was sharp, angry.

She drew back, and his expression softened. "Really, I fell," he said. "I probably had too much to drink." He pulled a wallet from his pocket, opened it and thrust a sheaf of bills at her.

She stared at the wad of twenties—at least two hundred dollars. "This is too much," she protested.

"Go on. Take it. You're always so good with Jackson, and he's crazy about you. In fact, could you come again next Friday night? I have to go out again."

"Of course." She was still staring at the money, afraid to look at his damaged face again.

"Now go on," he said. "I'll be fine." He moved past her, and she stared at his back, still frozen in place. At the bottom of the steps, he turned toward her once more. "No need to tell anyone about this," he said. "It would be too embarrassing."

"Of course not," she said. The last thing she wanted was to embarrass this man who had been so nice to her.

"Go home now, Lily," he said, and even smiled, though at the cost of a fresh trickle of blood from his swollen lip. "I'll be fine. I'll wait and set the alarm as soon as you're out."

She pocketed the money, collected her things, and let herself and Shelby out. In the six years she had known Denny Endicott, he had never been anything but perfectly polished and calm. She had never seen him even tipsy. Had never smelled alcohol on him. She had looked up to him, as a kind of father figure even.

But he was only human, and humans did drink too much. They fell down. But who got a black eye and a busted lip from a fall? And why hadn't the clients he had been entertaining made sure his injuries were treated?

But it was none of her business. Though she thought of Denny Endicott as her friend, he operated in a world far removed from her own. His problems involved billions of dollars and how to raise his son as a single father.

All she had to do worry about was training her dog, doing her job as a ski patroller and dealing with an exacting boss. It was enough for any one person—right?

"WE'LL DO SHELBY'S Level B certification tomorrow before the lifts open," Scott informed Lily after morning meeting the next Thursday. "Be at the back bowl off of Lift 12 at seven a.m."

Lily wanted to protest this was a waste of everyone's time, but she knew that wouldn't get her anywhere. "All right," she said.

Shelby had aced her first Level B test, less than eight months ago. There was no reason to think she wouldn't do well this time, either, unless Scott had done something to make the test harder. Did he resent Lily's presence on the team so much he would engineer her failure? She shook her head. Even if Scott had been reluctant to have her as part of his group, he hadn't done anything to make her think he was that vindictive.

So Friday morning found her and Shelby at the appointed location a few minutes before 7:00 a.m. The sun had barely risen over the ridge, casting long shadows over the pristine snow. Lily's teeth chattered, and she swung her arms and stamped her feet, trying to generate warmth.

A tall figure skied up beside her and skid to a stop, snow flying. Fellow patroller Nina Rose grinned at Lily as she stepped out of her skis. "Are you ready for this?" she asked.

"We're ready." Lily tried not to feel self-conscious around Nina, but she, along with everyone else she knew, had been glued to their televisions the last winter Olympic games. They had all seen Nina claim a silver medal in the giant slalom. A few months later she had graced the cover of *Vanity Fair*, wearing a whisper of a gown that showed off her athletic figure.

Nina looked past Lily. "Here comes everyone else."

Lily turned, expecting to see Scott and maybe one other person he had recruited to serve as a judge for this test. Instead, she was startled to see all of the other dog handlers—

Brian, Anders and Connor skied up just ahead of Scott. “I didn’t expect to see you all here so early,” she said.

“We came to cheer you and Shelby on,” Connor said.

Scott skied up with a tall man dressed all in black, a full ginger beard obscuring most of his face. “Hello, Lily,” Adam Derocher said. “How are you?”

“I’m good,” she said. “It’s good to see you.” She meant the words—Adam had been one of her trainers with C-RAD.

“We’re all here. Let’s get started,” Scott said, without preliminaries. “Adam will be the judge. Lily, are you and Shelby ready?”

“We’re ready.” She ignored the flutter in her stomach. Shelby had performed well at every trial so far, but she was still a young dog. If she wasn’t in the mood to work this morning, they could end up embarrassed in front of friends and people she respected. Not to mention they would probably be kicked off the avy dog team.

Adam stepped forward. “Who are our volunteers?”

A man and a woman held up their hands. “This is Marion and Pete,” Scott said. “They live here in town and volunteered to be our victims this morning.”

“Great,” Adam said. “We’ll get a couple of people to show you what to do.”

Connor and Nina left with the couple. After the lifts closed yesterday they had dug snow caves where the volunteers would wait for Shelby to find them. Despite the cold and discomfort involved, there was no shortage of other resort employees and townspeople who were willing to volunteer to be buried in the snow for training exercises or certification tests like this one.

“We’ll run the obedience test while we wait,” Adam said.

“Sure.” Lily called Shelby to her side. The dog sat, eyes bright, ears up, the picture of attentiveness.

Lily ran through all the basic obedience commands—sit, stay, lie down, heel and come. "She can fetch, shake hands and bow, if you want to see those," she volunteered.

"Nah, that's good." Adam marked the paper on his clipboard. "Let's go see if the others are ready."

Anders and Brian met them halfway across the wide bowl. "Everything's set," Brian said. "Let's see Shelby do her stuff."

The dog danced around, clearly sensing something was up. Lily asked her to sit and she did, though she practically vibrated with anticipation. "You know the drill," Adam said. "The dog has to find two buried volunteers within twenty minutes." He consulted his watch. "The time is seven ten. She has until seven thirty."

Lily took a deep breath. This was it. The snowfield they were in was the size of a football field. The two volunteers could be hidden anywhere in this expanse of white. "Shelby?"

The dog fixed her gaze on Lily. "Go find!"

Shelby faced the snow, but didn't move. Lily's heart sank. She was about to give the command a second time when the dog took off, racing across the field, snow flying behind her.

Lily ran after the dog, aware of the others behind her. Shelby had her nose to the ground, "casting" back and forth for scent. Unlike search-and-rescue dogs, avalanche dogs weren't trained to fix on one particular person's scent. Rather, they detected any human scent and focused in on it. Supposedly, they could smell a person buried even thirty or forty feet deep.

Shelby let out a bark and began digging. Moments later a hand stuck up from the snow and waved. "Time, six minutes," Adam said.

Lily laughed and rushed to pet Shelby as others pulled Marion from the pit where she had been hiding.

"Good girl!" Marion declared, and hugged Shelby.

"One more to find," Adam reminded them.

"Shelby, go find!" Lily said.

Shelby took off again. She sniffed around Marion's hiding place for a few minutes, then moved farther away. Lily made her hands into fists and tried not to think about the time passing as the dog searched, but found nothing.

"Five minutes." Adam said.

Lily's stomach was in knots. *Come on!* she silently encouraged her dog. *You can do this.*

"Three minutes."

Lily turned to glare at Adam. His countdown wasn't helping.

A bark, then a shout from Brian. Shelby was all the way across the field. Lily hurried to the location as the dog dug frantically. Adam jogged up to her side. "Only one minute left," he said.

Just then, the snow collapsed in front of the dog and Pete poked his head out. "Good girl!" he cried, and patted the dog, who continued to dig at the snow.

"We'll take it from here," Brian said, and gently moved the dog aside and began digging out the grinning volunteer.

Lily took a well-worn rope toy from her pack. Shelby barked and leaped at the toy, then tugged hard in her favorite game—her reward for a job well done.

"Congratulations. You passed." Lily looked up to see Scott standing beside her. "I was a little worried there at the end, but Shelby came through."

"She was great," Lily said.

"Good job," Scott said. "Now let's get to work."

He headed for the lift. Adam moved in where Scott had

been standing. "I think Scott was more nervous than you were," he said.

"Why would he be nervous?" she asked.

"Probably because he knew if Shelby failed the certification, he'd have to remove you from the program. He didn't want to do that."

She wasn't sure she believed that. "I suppose it would look bad to lose me when I just joined the team," she said.

"I don't know anyone who takes this work more personally," Adam said. "Frankly, I'd love to have him on my team. But whenever I've asked about hiring him, he talks about how much this program means to him. Anyway, congratulations. Shelby did great. You should be proud. How old is she now?"

"Sixteen months."

"She should be ready for her Level A test by the time she's eighteen months. That's the minimum age we can certify her."

"I'll be in touch." She shook the hand he offered, then put on her skis and headed back toward the base area.

She was greeted by a chorus of "Congratulations!" when she entered patrol headquarters, and Shelby received plenty of pats on her way to her kennel.

"Settle down, everyone," Scott called. "We've got a lot on our schedule today."

And that was it. Another accomplishment ticked off, but just another day on the job. Maybe she and Jackson could raise a toast when she babysat for him tonight.

The rest of the day was a typical busy day. The snow was good and the sun was out, so the resort was packed. Lily helped transport a woman with a knee injury from a steep black run on the back side of the resort to the clinic at the base area, helped move a bunch of fencing to a storage area behind the terrain park, answered questions from tourists, took Shelby out for some exercise and obedience drills, and ran general patrols.

When she stopped for lunch at twelve thirty, she saw she had missed a call from Denny Endicott. He had left a voicemail. "We won't need you to babysit tonight. Change of plans. Thanks."

She wished she had been able to talk to him. She wanted to know how he was doing. But maybe he would have thought she was being too personal. She thought of him as a friend but really, to him she was probably just the babysitter.

She was collecting her belongings at the end of the day when Nina stopped by her locker. "Big plans for tonight?" Nina asked. She had freed her long blond hair from the braid she usually wore, and it fell about her face in attractive waves. She looked runway-ready in black leggings and a black turtleneck that accentuated every curve.

"I was supposed to babysit, but that got canceled," Lily said.

"Then come out with me. We can celebrate Shelby's certification."

At the mention of her name, the dog nuzzled Nina's hand. Nina obliged by rubbing the dog's ears.

"Where would we go?" Lily asked.

"Just to the Trail's End for a few drinks and something to eat. Nothing fancy. Some of the other patrollers will probably be there. The dogs will be fine here for the few hours we're gone. You can ride with me."

"Thanks. I'd like that. Just give me a sec." Though she had been part of this ski patrol team for a month now, she hadn't socialized much after work. It would be good to have a night out and get to know people better.

Chapter Three

The Trail's End was a popular hangout for locals and tourists alike, and on a Friday night it was packed with people, all talking loudly to be heard over the mix of alternative country that blared over the speakers. Scott pushed his way toward the bar, behind Connor and a lift tech named Hank. The two friends had waylaid Scott outside Ski Patrol headquarters and persuaded him to go out with them for a beer.

While they waited for the bartender, Hank entertained them with an account of the twelve-year-old triplets in matching pink ski suits and blond pigtails who had delighted the crowds in the lift lines by blowing bubbles and handing out candy to celebrate their birthday. "Cutest little girls, and they were eating up the attention, too," he said.

"Hey, it's our turn." Connor pointed to the bar, and they moved forward to place their orders.

Beer in hand, Scott turned to survey the crowd. He recognized a couple of fellow employees from the resort, as well as a few couples he had spotted on the slopes that day. Then the door opened and Nina entered. The tall blonde couldn't help but turn heads. Behind him, Hank gave a low whistle. "Our own Powder Princess," he said softly, a reference to a nickname some sports blog had given Nina in her ski racing days.

But it was the woman behind Nina who made Scott's heart strike an extra beat. Lily wasn't especially tall, but she carried herself with a confidence he admired. But she wasn't arrogant. People liked Lily, from the ski school toddlers to entitled tourists. Whereas he apparently had a talent for rubbing people the wrong way, Lily could charm even the grumpiest complainer.

He wouldn't say she had exactly charmed him, but she did distract him. He'd like to figure out why.

"Hey, Nina! Lily! Over here!" Connor raised one arm and motioned the women over.

"Hello, Connor. Hank. Scott." Lily's smile sent warmth through him, even though she had barely glanced at him.

The bartender approached. "What can I get you ladies?"

"Hah!" Hank said. He was a wiry dark-haired man with soulful brown eyes and a thin moustache. "I had to wait fifteen minutes to place my order."

Nina smiled at the bartender. "I'll have an Avalanche Pale Ale and an order of chili cheese fries." She glanced at Lily. "Is that okay? We can split the fries."

"Sure. I'll have a Snowcap Cider."

"My treat," Hank said, and reached for his wallet.

"No thanks," Nina said. "I always pay my own way." She handed over a credit card, the smile just as warm.

Lily handed over cash to cover her share of the order, then turned her back to the bar. She surveyed the crowd, then glanced at Scott. "Is everything okay?" she asked.

"Sure. Why wouldn't it be?"

"You're staring at me." She brushed a lock of golden-brown hair out of her eyes. "I thought maybe something was wrong."

He looked away. He hadn't meant to stare. He just had a hard time keeping his eyes off of her.

But he wasn't the only person in the bar focused on Lily. "Do you know that guy over there?" he asked, and gestured toward the cash register by the door, where a beefy middle-aged man had his gaze fixed on her.

She looked in the direction he had indicated, then straightened. "Mike?"

The man moved toward them. "Hey, Lily!" he said. He glanced at Scott.

"Um, this is Scott. Scott, this is Mike." No explanation of their relationship. Relative? Friend? Boyfriend? He must be at least fifteen years older than Lily, but some women had a thing for older guys. "How are you, Mike?"

"I'm okay." He moved in closer and lowered his voice. "I guess Denny got in touch with you?"

Scott angled away slightly and pretended not to listen. But it was impossible not to hear everything they said in these close quarters. And the name Denny intrigued him. Denny as in Denton Endicott?

"He left me a voicemail saying he didn't need me to babysit tonight," Lily said. "Is something wrong?"

"No. Not that I know of. The meeting just got canceled at the last minute. I just wondered what he said to you last week. About the shiner." He pointed to his eye.

"He said he drank too much and fell."

"That's what he told me, too," Mike said.

He didn't sound convinced. "He looked really rough when he came in that night," Lily said. The bartender set her drink on the bar, but she made no move to pick it up. "His jacket was torn—like he'd been in a fight."

Denton Endicott in a fight? Scott sipped his beer and pretended to be watching a couple on the dance floor. Tourists, who had clearly drunk too much. They were executing a series of dips and spins Scott bet would have at least one of them falling flat before the song was over. Meanwhile, he could clearly hear Lily's conversation with Mike.

"That doesn't sound like Denny," Mike said. "I mean, I've known him twenty years, and he's never been in a fight."

"What about the client he was with that night?" Lily asked. "Do you know him? Or her?"

"Him. And he's a great guy. Someone else I've known for years. No, it must have been a fall." He laughed. "Denny and I are both getting older. We don't hold our liquor like we used to."

"What about this new employee, Preston Smith?" she asked.

Mike's expression sobered. "How do you know Preston?"

"He came by the house that night, not long after you left. He said he wanted to speak to you. He got kind of annoyed when I wouldn't let him in."

"I'm sorry he bothered you. I had no idea."

"It's all right. I meant to say something to Denny about it, but then he came in looking so awful and it seemed silly. I mean, the guy didn't do anything. Did Smith ever get in touch with you?"

"Not that night, but we work together every day."

"What do you think of him?" she asked.

"He certainly knows his stuff, but I'm not sure he's a good fit for the organization," Mike said. "He's got an attitude."

"Why did Denny hire him?"

"He's got excellent credentials and came highly recommended." Mike shrugged. "As long as he does his work, I guess his personality doesn't matter. I'll tell him to stay away from the house, though. He shouldn't be showing up after hours like that."

"Mike?" a server, holding a brown paper bag, called from the cash register.

"My order's up. I'd better go." He nodded and left.

Lily turned back to the bar and picked up her drink.

Scott moved in closer once more. On his other side, Nina was deep in conversation with Hank and Connor. "Everything okay?" he asked.

She frowned, a single shallow line forming on her forehead. "I hope so. Mike works for Denton Endicott. I was supposed to babysit Jackson again tonight, but his dad called at the last minute to cancel. When I was there last Friday, Denny came in from his dinner meeting with a black eye." She set her drink on the bar and turned to face him. "And I just remembered I promised Denny not to say anything to anyone about that, so if you tell anyone, I swear I'll make you regret it for the rest of your life."

He might have laughed at the threat, coming from such a sweet-faced young woman. But the vehemence with which she spoke gave weight to the words. "I won't say a word," he said. "I promise." And he wouldn't ask about Preston Smith, either, who had apparently annoyed her enough that she thought him worth mentioning to Mike. None of Scott's business.

She picked up her drink again and sipped. "Let's talk about something else," she said.

"Shelby made it interesting for us today," he said. "I was getting worried she wasn't going to find Pete in time."

"I had faith in her," Lily said.

He thought she had looked a little panicked, but whatever. The dog had come through and passed the exam, and that's all that mattered.

"I know you think I was singling you out, insisting you

recertify," he said. "But we can't afford to have any of our qualifications questioned. Better to be certain."

"You're the boss," she said. "You don't owe me an explanation."

The dismissal hurt, he could admit it. He didn't like that she thought of him first as "the boss." "I'm in charge of the avy dog program," he said. "But we're all part of the team. It's important that we get along."

She sipped her cider, watching him over the rim of the glass. She had almond-shaped eyes with thick lashes. Her gaze struck him as…troubled. Not what he had expected. "It's a good team," she said. "I don't have any problems with anyone."

"Good. I don't want any problems."

"What do you want?"

The question startled him. It sounded like a challenge. Did she expect him to tell her what he required from her, as a member of his team? But he had given her that spiel her first day on the job. "I want the avalanche dog program to be a success," he said.

"Because then you'll be a success. You'll keep your job."

"No!" The word came out more sharply than he had intended. She visibly flinched. "If someone is caught in a slide, they're depending on us to get them out alive," he added. "That's the only success that really matters."

Her eyes grew glossy, as if she was holding back tears. "You're right," she said, her voice rough. "Of course that's what matters most."

He hadn't expected so much emotion and had to look away. Awkward silence stretched between them.

"I'm going to head out of here." Connor clamped one hand on Scott's shoulder and smiled at Lily. "Have a good night."

"Good night, Connor." Lily set her half-finished drink on the bar. Scott was sure she was going to cry off, too, if only to get away from him.

But Nina moved in beside her and shoved a plate piled with chili cheese fries toward her. "Eat up," she said, and handed Lily a fork. "Or else I'll devour them all."

Lily hesitated, then stabbed the fork into the fries. Scott didn't blame her: the food looked and smelled amazing.

Hank moved over to flirt more with Nina, and Nina shut him down with practiced finesse. Scott said nothing, but continued to watch Lily while trying to appear not to. He told himself he should leave, but he couldn't bring himself to do that, any more than he could bring himself to move away from her.

"We should go out somewhere nicer than this," Hank said. He grimaced. "Someplace quieter, where we can talk."

"I'm here with my friend Lily," Nina said. "We're celebrating a big accomplishment for her today."

"Lily can come, too," he said. "And Scott." He looked across the women to Scott. "You can come out, can't you?"

"Not tonight," Scott said. He set his empty beer bottle on the counter. "Some of us have to be at work early in the morning."

"I'd better go, too," Lily said. "I can call an Uber to take me back to my place."

"If you're sure you don't mind," Nina said.

"Does that mean you're up for going with me?" Hank asked.

Nina smiled. "Just for a few drinks. A game of pool, maybe."

"Sure. Sure. Just friends."

Lily bit back a smile. Scott had to fight back a laugh. Hank was as eager as a puppy.

"Is your car back at the resort?" Scott asked Lily.

"Shelby and I rode the shuttle in this morning." The free shuttle ran a continuous loop between 6:00 a.m. and 10:00 p.m. She checked her watch. "I don't think I'll make the last bus, though."

"I'll take you home then," he said. "Where do you live?"

"The Ridge condos."

"No problem. I live there, too." The Ridge was a big complex, with four sections of buildings.

"Oh. Well, we'll have to stop by patrol and collect Shelby."

"We can do that."

He led the way outside. "I didn't say that about having to be at work early as some dig at you," he said. "I don't care how long you stay out as long as you're on time in the morning."

"I didn't think you did," she said. "I just didn't want to go out with them."

He glanced at her. "Why not?"

She shrugged. "I wasn't interested. Why didn't you go out with them?"

"Same reason," he said. "I wasn't interested. I did the bar scene in college and when I first got out of the army, but I don't enjoy it now. I'd rather stay home with my dog. Guess that makes me boring."

"Then I'm boring, too. I was supposed to babysit tonight and I was actually looking forward to it. Pepperoni pizza, Dr Pepper, and the rom-com of my choice after the kid went to bed. And Shelby on the couch at my feet, snoring."

"Sounds like the perfect evening."

She laughed, and he joined in. Her low, husky chuckle set a tremor through his stomach that startled him. Yeah, that was definitely some heat there. No surprise. He liked women, and she was an attractive one. Smart and interesting. But not interested in him. She'd made that pretty clear.

The Scott Lily had seen tonight was different from the Scott she saw at work. Less uptight. Friendlier. He wasn't her boss after hours—he was just another guy. A good-looking, interesting guy.

And full of surprises. Instead of crossing the street to the parking lot, as she had expected, he stopped at the curb half a block down from the bar. "Here we are."

She stared at the black, brown and silver motorcycle parked at the curb. Clearly, the bike belonged to Scott—Hunter was standing in the side car, tail wagging. Scott patted the dog, then unlocked a compartment on the rear of the bike, took out a helmet and handed it to her.

"I didn't know you had a motorcycle," she said.

"The bike is easier than a car for getting around town. Cheaper, too." He donned his own helmet and straddled the bike, then looked back at her. "Is something wrong?"

"No. I'm fine." She shoved the helmet onto her head and fumbled with the latch.

"Come here," he beckoned, then reached out to fasten the helmet's strap. A shiver raced through her as his fingertips brushed the sensitive skin beneath her chin. She shook off the sensation and climbed on behind him, while Hunter settled into the sidecar.

"How are we going to get to my place with Shelby?" she asked.

"She can ride in the sidecar with Hunter. There's plenty of room."

He started the engine, and she steadied herself with one hand on his shoulder, aware of the hard muscle bunched beneath her palm. She put as much distance between them as possible—a scant two inches—gripped the seat beneath her thighs, and stifled a squeal when the bike rolled forward and into the street.

They sped through the darkened streets of the resort town. Once they turned off the main drag there were few people on the sidewalks. Cold air stung her cheeks, but the sensation of scenery flying by was exhilarating. Too soon, they turned into the ski resort. But instead of heading to the parking garage, Scott steered the bike down a series of alleys and passages and came out on the snow beside ski patrol headquarters. She was pretty sure he wasn't supposed to have a motorcycle there, but she didn't say anything. Maybe he wasn't the total rule-follower she had pegged him for.

He opened the door to ski patrol headquarters, and Shelby barked at them from her kennel at the back. Lily retrieved her, Scott locked up, and they headed outside again.

Hunter jumped out of the sidecar to greet Shelby, and the two dogs danced around each other. "Let's go, Hunter," Scott commanded.

The Lab hopped into the sidecar and looked up at Scott expectantly. "Get in, Shelby," Scott said.

Shelby looked up at him and wagged her tail.

"She doesn't know that command," Lily said.

Scott bent and scooped the dog into his arms. "Move over, Hunter," he said, and deposited Shelby in the sidecar next to Hunter. "Stay."

Shelby settled down next to Hunter, alert, but not upset. "Good girl," Lily said.

They mounted the bike again and set off. Shelby took her cues from Hunter and sat still, panting and glancing around her. Lily was less relaxed, the rumble of the motorcycle engine vibrating through her. Scott drove faster out on the highway. Lily tried to keep her balance by holding on to the seat, but ended up with her hands on Scott's waist, the rest of her pressed against his back.

The Ridge condos had been constructed ten years previously as affordable housing for workers. Most importantly, the complex allowed pets. Lily had been lucky to snag a vacant unit, though it was a single-bedroom space on the third floor. Still, she had great views and no upstairs neighbors, and it was enough for her and Shelby. "Which building are you in?" Scott asked as he slowed and turned the bike into the main entrance.

"Building Two," she said.

"I'm in Building One." He stopped the bike in the parking lot for Building Two. Lily dismounted, and Shelby sprang out of the sidecar after her.

"Thanks for the lift," Lily said.

"You did a good job today," Scott said. "With Shelby. If I didn't say so already. I'm not always good about that. Giving praise where it's due, I mean. I'm trying to do better."

"Um, thanks," she said. "That means a lot."

She started to turn away, but he called after her. "Don't forget my helmet."

"Oh. Sure." She fumbled again to unfasten the buckle, but her fingers seemed to have lost all dexterity.

Scott reached out and gently pushed her hands away, then unfastened the buckle himself. He lifted the helmet off her head, then reached out to smooth her hair.

The gesture was unexpected, almost tender, and sent a shiver of awareness through her. Which just proved how exhausted she really was. She took a step back. She had learned some things about Scott tonight—that he cared more than she gave him credit for. And that she was more attracted to him than she wanted to be.

THE NEXT DAY—Saturday—was the usual mixture of crowds and chaos. Lily scarcely had time to exchange a few words with the rest of the crew between morning meeting and heading up the slopes to begin work. She responded to three minor injuries before noon. She was starting up the mountain for a last run before lunch when she heard a familiar voice hail her as she waited to board the lift to Top of the Mark. Jackson Endicott skied up to her. He was dressed in black pants, a blue jacket and a black helmet plastered with stickers form the various resorts he had skied. "Can I ride up with you?" he asked.

"Sure." She moved over to make room, and they skied forward when the liftie waved to them.

"How's your dad doing?" Lily asked when they were on the lift chair.

"Have you seen his eye?" Jackson swiveled toward her.

She pretended ignorance. "What happened to his eye?"

"He tripped and fell coming out of the restaurant last Friday. He's got a black eye that looks like something out of a horror movie—all green and purple and yellow. I told him it would make a great Halloween costume."

"Is he okay?" she asked.

"Oh yeah. He's here somewhere." He waved a hand to take in the resort. "I'm supposed to meet him for lunch." He turned back to her. "How's Shelby?"

"Shelby's great. She passed her Level B certification test yesterday."

He frowned. "Is that like, a math test or something?"

"It's a test of how well she can find people buried in the snow. She had to find two people within twenty minutes, and she did it."

"That's great. If I was buried in the snow, do you think she could find me?"

"I bet she could. But don't go burying yourself to see."

"Okay." They approached the top of the lift, and he faced forward. "See you!" he shouted as he sped away.

She spent the rest of the day patrolling at the terrain park and beginner areas, took Shelby out for a patrol midday, and did a safety demonstration—with Shelby's help—for a ski school class. She kept an eye out throughout the day for Denny or Jackson Endicott, but saw neither of them. The image of Denny, torn jacket and beaten face, stuck with her.

The radio attached to her pack strap crackled to life. "All patrollers report to patrol base," Scott's voice was urgent. "I need you here now."

Lily straightened her line and crouched over her skis in a racing stance. She sped past Shelby, who barked and ran after her. She crested the hill above the base and slowed only slightly to avoid the clusters of tourists lingering at the bottom of the run, and skidded to a stop outside the door marked Patrol.

As she was stepping out of her skis, Chase, Connor and Livi Rasmussen—known to all as Raz—arrived. "What's going on?" Chase asked.

"No idea," Connor said, and the others shook their heads as well.

Inside the patrol office Anders Iverson, handler of the team's second black Labrador retriever, Darth, was pulling out stainless steel dog dishes and filling them from one of the barrels, a half circle of attentive dogs focused on his every move.

Scott stopped Lily just inside the door. "Have you seen Jackson Endicott this afternoon?" he asked.

"Jackson? I rode up to Top of the Mark with him before lunch, but I haven't seen him since."

"You haven't even caught sight of him in the distance on a run or while riding the lift?" Scott asked.

"No. Why?"

Scott looked at the other patrollers. "Do any of the rest of you know Jackson Endicott? Nine years old, a little over four feet tall, sixty-nine pounds, light brown hair and blue eyes. He's wearing black ski pants and a blue Spider jacket and a black ski helmet. Atomic skis."

The very precise description alarmed Lily. "What's going on?" she asked.

"Have any of you seen a kid like that this afternoon?" Scott asked.

The others shook their heads. Lily tugged on Scott's arm. "What's going on?" she asked again. "Has something happened to Jackson?"

His gaze met hers, worry deepening the lines at the corners of his eyes. "He's missing. Someone reported seeing him going through the backcountry gates a little before three o'clock. He hasn't been seen since."

Chapter Four

"Jackson is a good skier, but he knows he's not supposed to ski out of bounds." Denton Endicott was a big, burly man with a football linebacker's build and a slight paunch. Incongruously, he also sported a black eye, the bruising faded to a yellowish-green. Though the pictures Scott had seen of him in the media depicted a powerful, commanding presence, worry for his only child had diminished him, hunching his shoulders and reducing his voice to a hoarse croak. "He's never even asked to ski that terrain before," he continued.

"We're sending every patroller on duty to search for him right now," Scott said. "The dogs will search, too."

"Shelby knows him," Lily said. "She'll recognize him right away."

Scott didn't hide his annoyance at her interruption. "All the dogs are trained to seek out human scent," he said. "They'll key in on Jackson, even if he's fallen or in an area where he's hard to see."

"When did you last see your son, Mr. Endicott?" The questioner was Sheriff Van Howard. Denton Endicott had called him in immediately after telling the resort about his concerns for his son. Scott imagined that hadn't gone over very well with the resort's top brass. They would have preferred to keep bad news from the public if at all possible. Even if Jackson had disobeyed his father and headed off-piste, there was a good chance the patrollers would locate him. The resort was big, but it wasn't that big.

"We skied together down May Day right after lunch," Endicott said. "I had a meeting, so I left Jackson to ski on his own. He's been skiing since he was three and knows the resort as well as I do. He often skis by himself or with friends."

"Was he with friends this afternoon?" the sheriff asked.

"No. He told me he was going to go over to the terrain park and play around there for a while."

The terrain park was located off of Daisy Chain, halfway between Top of the Mark and Lift Four. Daisy Chain was also the closest run to the gates leading to the hike-to, inbound terrain. Those gates closed at 3:00 p.m.

"A lift tech reported a boy who fit Jackson's description passing through the gate near Daisy Chain a few minutes before three," Scott said.

"We got there right at three to secure the gate, and the liftie told us about it," Chase said. Beside him, Raz nodded in agreement.

"You didn't try to stop him?" Endicott asked.

"It's not illegal to go through the gate before three o'clock," Chase said. His normally sallow face was flushed, his light brown eyes troubled.

"Was Jackson by himself?" Lily asked.

"The liftie didn't see anyone else," Chase said.

"That gate serves all the terrain in Creek Bowl." Scott indicated a shaded area on the map on the wall behind him. "I'm going to assign a segment of the bowl to each patroller. We'll do a thorough sweep of the area. If Jackson is there, we'll find him."

When they exited the patrol office, dusk was already staining the sky purple and casting long shadows across the snow. With the lifts shut down, they had to snowmobile up the mountain. Chase clapped Lily on the back. "You and Shelby ride with me," he said, and headed toward the row of snowmobiles beside the office.

They stowed their skis on the back, then Lily straddled the seat and Shelby balanced in front of her. While the dog was a pro at riding the lifts or even being transported down the mountain in a sled, she was skittish on the snowmobiles, constantly shifting her weight and trying to find a comfortable position. Lily grabbed the handle on the back of her harness and held on, steadying her as Chase gunned the machine up the mountain.

At the top, Lily clicked into her skis and joined the others standing at the gate—really just a gap in the ropes marking the boundary between lift-served terrain and inbounds backcountry. A large sign informed anyone contemplating passing through this gap of the dangers of skiing off-piste. The patrollers studied the snow, with lines of ski tracks cutting through the powder at the edge of the drop into the big bowl of terrain that swept down toward a forest of trees. Just beyond those trees was the dividing line between the resort and the national forest from which SkyCrest leased terrain. Ropes and signs along this line declared Ski Area Boundary.

"We should look in the trees," Anders said. "It would be easy to get tangled up in there, or turned around." He didn't add that tree skiing presented hazards such as hitting a tree at high speed or falling into the well created when snow collapsed around the tree's roots, but everyone thought about that. They wanted to find Jackson alive, but they had to be prepared for the worst.

Next to Anders, Darth danced impatiently, then let out a short, sharp bark.

"Let's go," Anders said, and skied through the gate and dropped into the bowl. Darth, still barking, raced after him.

The others followed, skiers and dogs spreading out across the terrain that looked smooth and pristine from above, but in reality was rough in places, icy in others, and full of deep, soft powdery snow in others. The fading daylight made it difficult to see variations in terrain, and Lily bent her knees more deeply to avoid being thrown off balance. "Jackson!" she shouted as she reached the edge of the trees.

Shelby darted between the silvered trunks of aspens and bounded over downed trees and boulders. Lily guided her skis in the narrow alleys between trees, sometimes following the tracks of those who had passed through here earlier in the day, sometimes carving her own route. "Jackson!" she called, over and over until her voice was hoarse and her throat was sore.

She kept her radio turned up, positioned high on the strap of her pack where she would be sure to hear it, certain that at any moment one of her fellow patrollers would radio that the boy had been found. Maybe he had fallen and hurt himself, or maybe he had become lost in the trees. Or maybe he had left this bowl long ago and was back at the family's chalet, drinking hot chocolate and unaware of the fuss he had caused.

She was wondering if she should put on her headlamp when the radio finally crackled. "Return to base, everybody," Scott ordered.

Lily keyed her mic. "Have they found Jackson?" she asked.

"Negative, but it's getting too dark to search. Someone is going to get hurt."

She wanted to protest, but here in the trees she could hardly see two feet in front of her. More than once she had had to extricate herself from a snow-covered pile of branches. She was shivering from the cold, and Shelby plodded along beside her, tongue hanging out, clearly spent.

But first they had to climb up out of the bowl. She found the track used by those who braved the area during the day. Connor and Raz were there, clicking out of their skis. Chase and Anders, with Darth, were climbing ahead of them. Lily shouldered her skis and whistled for Shelby. Bent forward, she began the hike up to the lifts, kicking the toes of her boots into the icy snow, following the rough stairs made by the skiers who had climbed out of the bowl before her.

Scott was waiting at the gate, Hunter stretched out on the snow at his side. As each patroller passed through, they moved to the side and clicked back in their skies, then waited, until everyone was accounted for. "Any word on the boy?" Anders asked.

"Nothing." Scott looked grim. "The resort is sending up a helicopter first thing in the morning to do an aerial search. This area will remain closed tomorrow. We're going to have someone at the gate all day to enforce the closure. Everyone go home now. Try to get some sleep. We're back on at five."

Lily was so cold she could no longer feel her fingers and toes, and her legs ached. But she still had to ski down to the base. She squatted down. "Are you ready, Shelby?" she asked.

Shelby was always ready. She jumped into Lily's arms, then scrambled up onto her shoulders. Lily stood, made sure she and the dog were balanced, and skied down. The other patrollers with dogs assumed the same posture. This was one of the first things Shelby had learned in her preparation to be an avalanche dog. Running long distances on snow was hard on a dog's joints, especially when they were already tired, either from a search or from patrolling all day.

Sometimes they were taken down the mountain on snowmobiles, or in sleds, but carrying them down was often the most expedient mode of transport.

"Watch your claws," Lily said, as one of Shelby's back paws dug into her neck. She put up a hand to a furry haunch. Shelby was a lot bigger now than when Lily had trained her as a pup, but she didn't mind. No matter what kind of day she had had, ending it with her dog literally wrapped around her was comforting.

But even Shelby couldn't completely console her this evening. What had happened to Jackson? He was such an appealing combination of smart and naive, daring and timid. Not being able to find him filled her with dread. Already the temperature was below freezing, and weather reports called for up to six inches of snow. A little boy alone out there was in real danger of freezing to death.

She and Shelby had trained for months in order to save lives. She felt so helpless now, not being able to do anything.

SCOTT GAVE UP trying to sleep at 3:00 a.m. He went out at three thirty to shovel a path to the street. As predicted, about five inches of soft snow now blanketed the area. The motorcycle wasn't ideal for these conditions, but he had good tires and would take it slow. Fortunately, he didn't have far to go. The temperature was sitting at zero, which would make for an uncomfortable ride. He tried to avoid thinking of the little boy who had spent the night out in this, but his mind kept returning to the memory of Denton Endicott, distraught over his son's disappearance.

By four fifty he was unlocking the door of the patrol office. Hunter trotted in after him and began sniffing his empty food dish. "It's not breakfast time yet," Scott told him, then fished a jerky treat from his pocket and passed it over. Satisfied, Hunter took the treat to a dog bed along the wall to eat.

Ten minutes later, the resort operations manager, Doug Elam, entered the office. Fifty, with dark hair just graying at the temples and the chiseled features of a movie star, Elam was the third generation of his family to head Sky-Crest resort. When the property had sold to Brugenhoff Resorts five years before, Elam had been part of the deal and had continued to guide operations ever since. "I saw your light," he said.

"Any news?" Scott asked.

"We built a bonfire in Creek Bowl last night," Doug said. "Figured the boy might see it and make his way to it. His dad and some other family spent the night out there. I think they might still be there, but I haven't heard anything."

"The sheriff said the helicopter would be here first light," Scott said.

"As long as the snow stops," Doug said. He moved to stand beside the desk where Scott sat. "What have you got on tap this morning?"

"We'll hit the usual trouble spots with charges," Scott said. "That cornice on Baker Ridge builds up in weather like this. We'll want to make sure to bring it down before we open the runs below it. And we have to hit the slopes above Buttermilk Basin and Tessa's Trees. We usually mitigate in Creek Bowl, too, but I think we need to hold off on that for now. Especially since the area is closed."

"Right." Neither of them mentioned they didn't want to bury the kid's body, if it was there.

"Nobody goes into that area without a beacon, though," Scott said. "There's not a big slide risk on those slopes, but there's some."

"You've got six dogs who can find people without beacons," Doug said.

"They can, but do you want to be the seventh person under the snow if a slide lets loose?"

"You know I just like to give you a hard time," Doug said.

Scott glared. Though Doug had declared himself in favor of the avalanche dog program at SkyCrest, Scott knew he was getting pressure from people higher up in the organization to cut the expensive, and what they saw as unnecessary, program.

Voices approaching drew his attention. The door to the office opened and patroller Nina Rose walked in, her red golden retriever, Sky, prancing beside her. Nina was SkyCrest's biggest celebrity, and Scott had worried fans would distract her from her work with ski patrol, but it turned out that the ski patrol uniform—complete with helmet and goggles—rendered her anonymous, which she seemed to prefer.

"Lily called and told me last night about the missing little boy," Nina said as she patted Hunter, who had come forward to greet her and Sky. She hadn't worked the day before, but it didn't surprise Scott that she already knew what was going on. Theirs was a small, close community.

"How is Lily doing?" Doug asked. He directed the question at Scott.

"She's fine," Scott said. He had already voiced his objections to Doug when Lily was hired—mainly, that he had had no say in her selection or training. Doug had made it clear that he was obligated to take in any Kingdom Mountain employees who wanted jobs with SkyCrest.

Two other patrollers—David Reagan and Trey Manuel—had also transferred from Kingdom Mountain, but they were different. They didn't have dogs. Scott had put his job on the line to lobby for formation of the avalanche dog program, and one screwup—say, by a person with a poorly trained dog—could bring the ax down on what Doug still referred to as an experiment. But he didn't think Lily was going to be that screwup. "She's working out okay," he added.

The door opened again, and Lily and Shelby entered. The dog made a beeline for Scott and shoved her nose right between his legs.

"Hey!" he yelled, and pushed her away.

"She likes you," Nina said, stifling laughter.

Lily's face was red. "Come here, Shelby," she said. "Don't be such a goof."

"I'd better not catch her doing that to a guest," Scott said.

Lily turned away, fussing with the straps on her pack, and once again he regretted being so quick to rebuke her. Why did he find it so difficult to relax around her?

One by one, the rest of the team reported for duty—not merely the patrollers who were scheduled to work that day, but all of them. "I figured I could help look for the boy," Brian Weeks, who with his golden retriever, Daisy, was supposed to be off this week, said. Part-timers Carson Slade and Charli Castro arrived, too.

"We're waiting for a report from the helicopter that's doing an aerial search this morning," Scott told them. "In the meantime, everyone can help with mitigation."

A murmur of agreement. This was active work that required concentration—just the thing to keep their minds off the missing child. Scott handed out assignments, and they prepared to exit patrol headquarters. Scott left them with his familiar parting words, "Be careful out there."

THE PATROLLERS SPLIT into teams, each assigned a different area. Lily and Connor were together this morning, their dogs kenneled at headquarters while they hauled backpacks full of explosive charges—essentially grenades—up the mountain via snowmobile to lob onto any slopes that might be holding snow. Other teams would ride up to bomb other slopes, while still others would take to the air in the resort's helicopter to reach high-angle slopes that would otherwise be inaccessible.

Over the more than fifty years SkyCrest had been in operation, generations of patrollers had learned the tendencies of the snow in every area of the resort. But the constantly changing weather and terrain required continual reassessment. At Top of the Mark, Connor and Lily dug snow pits to assess the characteristics of the snow. They consulted records and their own memories to determine what kind of charges they should use and where they should target them for the best effect.

They were setting their final charges of the day when a helicopter skimmed overhead, Forest Service green stripes clear on its side. "I hope they find the little guy," Connor said as he and Lily watched the chopper disappear from view.

"I hope they find him alive," Lily said.

The lower slopes had to be cleared before the lifts started operating at 9:00 a.m. Higher elevations sometimes delayed opening if more time was needed to clear them, but the goal was to have everything open no later than 10:00 a.m. barring extreme storm conditions.

With so many extra hands, all the runs were open by nine. The patrollers spread out across the resort to post up at various lift shacks around the mountain. From there they would respond to calls for assistance from guests and their fellow employees. Sometimes they needed to set up ropes to keep people out of hazardous areas, or make an appearance to slow down speedy skiers. They gave directions, answered questions, and offered advice to guests, handed out avy dog trading cards and resort maps, and even posed for pictures. Their primary job was ensuring guest safety, but they were also there to be ambassadors for SkyCrest.

Lily reported back to the main patrol office at nine thirty to feed Shelby and take her out for a break. The dogs spent most of their days kenneled, with breaks to socialize and run around, or to run training drills, but their primary purpose was to be ready if needed.

Scott was on the phone when she entered the office, his face animated. When he wasn't frowning, he was a good-looking guy—strong jaw, cleft chin, intense hazel eyes. Though today those eyes were underscored with half-moon shadows, and his jaw was dusted with a day's growth of beard. "Just the single set of tracks? You're sure they don't belong to anyone who was at the bonfire last night? You really think it could be him? Of course I'll be right there. Two of us. With dogs."

He hung up the phone. "They've found something?" Lily asked.

"The helicopter saw a sets of ski tracks exiting the woods at the resort boundary line," he said. "The imprint was pretty shallow, and he thought it looked shorter than most adult skis." He stood and shrugged into his jacket.

"Shorter kids' skis," she said. "Less weight on the snow."

"That's what they're thinking." He grabbed an avalanche beacon from the cubby behind him and checked the battery level.

"The chopper is going to pick me up at heli-ski operations." He clipped on the beacon and grabbed his pack. "They lost the tracks when they went into the trees again. I'm taking Hunter. The helicopter can set us down near the tracks. With luck we can catch up with them. I'll radio Connor and Farley to meet us there and go with me."

Lily stepped in front of him, blocking his exit. "Take me and Shelby. Jackson knows us. He's been out all night by this time. He's probably terrified. A familiar face is going to make things easier on everyone."

He hesitated. "Have you trained for backcountry rescue?"

"Not wilderness search-and-rescue, but I've trained with C-RAD on avalanche rescue—search techniques and first aid."

"It's not the same as search-and-rescue."

He tried to move past her, but she remained where she was, refusing to give way. "Jackson knows me. If two men he doesn't know are out there calling for him, he's liable to be afraid. He might even hide from you."

He looked at Shelby, who was standing at the door of the kennel, poised to come out. "Has Shelby ridden a helicopter before?"

"Of course." This was a lie. They hadn't reached the level of training that included riding in helicopters. But she had faith in her dog. Shelby wasn't the type to freak out over anything.

"All right," he said. "But you have to keep up."

She released Shelby from her kennel and grabbed a beacon, then raced after Scott.

Chapter Five

Scott hadn't asked if Lily herself had ridden in a helicopter before. She hadn't thought it mattered, but now that they were inside the noisy beast, rising straight into the air while her stomach stayed on the ground, she was having second thoughts about volunteering for this mission.

She gritted her teeth and focused on not losing her breakfast. Shelby lay between Lily's feet, head up and ears back, but obedient to the command Lily had given her to stay.

Next to them, between Scott's feet, Hunter let out a high-pitched whine. "It's okay, boy." Scott patted the dog. He glanced at Lily. "He's never liked flying."

"Have the two of you flown a lot?" she asked.

"A few times."

"For avalanche rescue work?"

"Yeah. Nothing inbounds, but we've responded to several backcountry slides."

"Has Hunter found people who were buried?" She and Shelby had spent hours training with people who volunteered to be buried in snow caves and "rescued" by the dogs, but she had yet to participate in a real rescue effort.

"He has. He made his first find less than five minutes into his very first search."

She almost smiled at the pride in his voice. She got it.

Seeing your dog succeed was every bit as satisfying as achieving something yourself.

Scott glanced at her, his expression more sober now. “None of them were alive,” he said. “The people he found, I mean. Even though we got to them within half an hour in one case, we were still too late.”

“They tell us that in the training,” she said. *Most searches are body searches*, she remembered her first instructor saying.

“That’s just the reality of what we do,” he said.

“Dogs do make live finds sometimes,” she said. “There was a handler who spoke to us at my last WBR training class.”

“Was it Ed Hayes?” he asked.

“Yes. And his dog.”

“Xena. Yeah, I know him. Everybody knows Ed and Xena. Because he’s the only person most of us have ever met who did have a live find. Or at least one that wasn’t made immediately after the avalanche. Most of the time our dogs aren’t on scene that quickly.”

“Do you ever think about that?” she asked. “I mean, why we’re even doing this if the chances are so minuscule that we’ll save someone?”

“I think about it all the time,” he said. “Especially every time I have to justify requesting more money for people who think they’re just paying for patrollers to have an excuse to bring their dog to work each day.”

“What do you tell them?”

He looked down at Hunter, who was silent now and lying at Scott’s feet. “I point out that dogs are great PR. Customers love dogs. They love seeing them on the slopes. Then I tell them if there’s a chance to save even one life we should take it. And I tell them that every single person who has ever lost a loved one due to an avalanche would say the same."

She looked away, voice rendered useless by the tears that clogged her throat. But she would choke to death before she cried in front of Scott. So she dug her fingernails into her palms and looked straight ahead, staring at the back of the pilot's head and wondering how deep the snow would be where they were going.

SCOTT THOUGHT ABOUT Clark on days like today, all blue sky and deep powder. His best friend's idea of heaven was first tracks on snow as light as feathers. Clark whooped and hollered as he skimmed over the surface with all the speed and agility of a cheetah.

He was doing just that the last time Scott saw him, leaving lines in the snow like a swooping signature on clean white paper. One moment Scott was admiring the way Clark made it look so easy and listening to his friend's shouts echoing off the surrounding mountains, and the next he was watching in horror as the whole top of a mountain fell down on him, like a building toppling.

Clark was wearing an avalanche beacon, but Scott couldn't find the signal. Much later, they would discover the beacon had been torn from his body by the force of the avalanche. It was two days before they found him, after hundreds of hours of probing by dozens of volunteers.

A dog could have found him sooner. Maybe not soon enough to save his life, but it would have saved his family and friends two days of agony. Even that was worth something, wasn't it?

"Look down there!" the pilot shouted over the roar of the engines and rotors and pointed to their right. Scott leaned forward and craned to see out the right side of the aircraft.

There, as if a giant had dragged two fingers through cake frosting, was the clear outline of ski tracks, leading from the woods that marked the ski area border, across a clearing and into the national forest.

The chopper rose and circled back, then arced down to hover low to the far left of the tracks. "I can't land in this snow!" the pilot shouted. "You're going to have to throw out your gear and jump out after it."

Lily stared at him, wide-eyed. Scott picked up his skis and tossed them out the door. His pack followed, then her skis and pack. When he reached for Shelby, Lily finally sprang to action. "You're not *throwing* her anywhere," she said. Before he could say anything, she hoisted the dog into her arms, moved to the door, and jumped.

THE SNOW WAS deep and soft as a featherbed, but it still made for an awkward landing. Lily landed on her back, with Shelby sprawled across her. The dog scrambled away, and she sat up just in time to see Scott, with Hunter in his arms, make his exit. As soon as he hit the ground, the chopper rose again.

She got up and started collecting their gear. She had to dig for one ski, but they recovered everything, and within a few minutes she was upright and ready to go. She stomped her feet, making an even place to stand on her skis.

Scott skied up beside her. "I wasn't going to throw your dog," he said. "I wouldn't do that."

She nodded. One thing she did know about him was that he took care of his dog. "It got me out of the chopper in a hurry, anyway," she said. She looked around them. "Where are the tracks?" Except for the spot where they had landed, the landscape appeared to be a smooth expanse of white.

"This way." Scott started to follow the tree line east.

In a few minutes he stopped and pointed one pole at the line of ski tracks. Lily was startled at how faint they were. “Later in the day, they’ll be invisible in the sun,” he said. “It’s only the way the light is slanting right now that helps them stand out.”

They decided to flank the tracks, the better to keep them in sight, and set out. There was enough of a downhill slant to the terrain to help them navigate without much problem on skis, but the dogs had to fight the snow, porpoising through the deepest stashes. “They’re going to wear themselves out,” Lily said.

“Ski behind me,” Scott said. “The dogs can follow in our tracks.”

She fell in behind him, and they commanded the dogs to do the same. The canines still struggled at times, but the going was a little easier. The tracks they had been following led into another thick stand of trees. Scott slid in between two trunks, and Lily followed. They wound their way in and out, stopping from time to time to reorient and make sure they were still following the faint track.

“We’re almost out of the trees,” Scott said when they had been skiing about fifteen minutes.

Five minutes later, they emerged, then stopped and stared. Two sets of tracks extended across the snow in front of them.

“Is that the track we were following?” She pointed with one ski pole to the smaller, fainter lines on the left.

“I think so,” Scott said.

“Then who is that?” She indicated the second set of tracks—longer skis and deeper indentations, laid out scarcely a foot from the smaller, fainter tracks.

Scott looked back over his shoulder. “I don’t know. But I didn’t see any other tracks back there.”

“Neither did I,” she said. “Do we keep following them?”

"Let's backtrack and see if we can figure out where these came from."

They skied along the edge of the clearing and found the place where the second tracks emerged. Then they followed the trail back into the woods. The tracks wound in and out among the trees, sometimes crossing the boy's tracks, sometimes taking a different path. Lily was following Scott and almost collided with his back when he stopped suddenly. She lurched to one side to avoid running over his skis.

"What is it?" she asked.

"It's a campsite." He moved forward, and she was able to see around him. The snow was beaten down, and someone had built a lean-to covered with pine boughs, snow thick on top of the boughs. Directly in front of the lean-to was the remains of a campfire, a thin tendril of smoke rising from the ashes. "They must have been here last night," she said.

Scott leaned over and fished something bright yellow from the snow. A candy wrapper. He walked to the lean-to and looked inside. "Looks like a couple of people spent the night here," he said. "There are depressions in the snow."

He took out his radio and attempted to transmit, but all they could hear was static. "Let's get out from under these trees," he said, and skied past her.

She followed him away from the campsite. By the time she reached his side, he was talking on the radio. "I'm sure someone spent the night here. Two people. And the two sets of ski tracks look like a kid and an adult."

"We can try to get some other searchers into the area." Lily thought she recognized the voice of the sheriff. "But there's another storm cell headed this way. Forecasters are saying it could drop another three to five inches of snow."

"Let us follow the tracks a little farther," Scott said.

"They can't have left the camp very long ago. The ashes of the fire are still warm."

They set out once more. The two ski tracks traveled in an almost straight line across the snow, on a slope that grew progressively steeper. If not for the seriousness of their mission, Lily might have enjoyed the almost unblemished powder and the crisp air.

The two humans might have skied for hours, but they had to stop to water the dogs and give them something to eat. She and Scott drank from their water bottles and ate gorp and beef jerky. "Where do you think they're going?" she asked. "I mean, besides farther into the woods? Are there any roads out here?"

"I'd have to check on a map to be sure, but I think this is all designated wilderness. No roads. The only town is the ghost town of Pandora. I think there are some summer homes there, and a general store that operates in the summer months. But I'm pretty sure you have to cross two ridges to get there from here. Not an easy trip to make any time of year, but especially in winter."

"Jackson isn't strong enough to ski all day in this terrain," she said. "He's just a kid. And he's not especially big for his age."

"At least we know as long as he's moving, he's alive, and the exercise will keep him warmer." He stowed his water bottle and adjusted his pack. "Come on. You're right about a kid not being able to ski all day. And he'll ski slower. That should give us a chance to catch up with them."

"If someone found Jackson and decided to spend the night rather than try to make it back to the resort in the snowstorm, why didn't they turn around this morning and head for the resort?" she asked. "Why move farther away?"

"I don't know," Scott said. "Maybe they got confused? We'll have to ask them when we find them."

"What are we going to do if we see them?" Lily asked.

"I don't know," Scott said. "I guess that depends on how they act."

They hadn't gone much farther before it began to snow again—big flakes, drifting gently down at first, but gradually getting heavier and heavier, until it was like standing in a swirl of feathers. "Hurry," Scott said. "The snow is going to fill in the tracks."

Lily tried to hurry, but she was exhausted, and the snow clung to her goggles, so that she had to pause every few feet to wipe them clear. At last, Scott stopped. "I can't see the tracks anymore," he said.

"We have to stop, for the dogs' sake, if not our own," she said. Both dogs lagged behind now, tongues hanging out, fur coats caked with snow.

"You're right." He pulled out a water dish and filled it for the pups.

Lily looked around them. She had no idea where they were. Scott's radio popped and crackled. "Scott, are you there?"

"I'm here," Scott answered.

"Were you able to follow the tracks?" the sheriff asked.

"We were, until it started snowing hard. We can scarcely make out anything now."

"The storm came in faster than we expected," the sheriff said.

"I don't think there's anything more we can do out here right now," Scott said.

"Can they pick us up?" Lily asked. Now that she was standing still, she was shivering, and fatigue dragged at her, as if she were hauling a sled full of bricks behind her.

"The helicopter is grounded until the weather clears," the sheriff said.

Scott looked at her. "I heard," she said. "What are we going to do?"

"You can try to ski out," the sheriff said.

They both looked back the way they had come—the route was rough, and the last half of the journey would be uphill. "I can't do it," Lily said. "And I don't think the dogs can, either."

"We've got emergency supplies," Scott said. "We'll make camp and spend the night. In the morning we can decide on our next steps."

"Roger that. We'll be in touch."

Scott hooked the radio back onto his pack. Silence closed in around them. Snow had gathered on their shoulders and the tops of their helmets. "Come on," Scott said. "Let's ski back into the woods. We'll have more shelter there."

The woods were farther away than Lily remembered. "Tell me again why we didn't come out here on snowmobile," she said.

"It's a wilderness area," he said. "No motorized vehicle traffic allowed."

"Not even in an emergency?" she asked, her voice rising sharply on the last word.

"Maybe there wasn't time to get permission," Scott said.

She fell silent. There was no sense debating what they might have done. They needed to focus on getting through the night.

At last, they entered the trees. Immediately the brunt of the storm lessened. By silent consensus they avoided the camp where they believed Jackson and his companion had spent the night. Scott led them to a small clearing and stopped. "This looks good," he said.

They stood still for a moment, not speaking. The silence of the snowy woods closed around them, making her feel a million miles away from anyone else. If the loneliness of this place spooked her, what would it feel like to a little boy, so far from everyone he knew and loved?

Chapter Six

This was not how Lily wanted to spend the night. She was cold, tired and hungry. The thought of trying to sleep in the snow without even a sleeping bag made her want to cry. But worse yet was the thought of spending long, idle hours with Scott. They had gotten along well enough all afternoon, and the other night at the bar, but she couldn't shake the feeling that he was judging her, and she could never relax around him. He was so freaking calm and competent—anything she said or did wasn't going to be good enough.

But she wasn't going to tell him any of this. She wouldn't give him the opportunity to label her as a complainer. Instead, she looked him in the eye and said, "What can I do to help?"

"We need a fire, and we need shelter," Scott said. "I'll start the fire. See if you can find some dry wood." He knelt and began clearing snow from a patch of ground. Both dogs lay down to watch.

She turned in a slow circle. Everything was covered in snow. The few tree branches she spotted on the ground would be soaking wet.

"Look underneath trees and deeper in the undergrowth," Scott said, not looking up. He had taken out a knife and was shaving a twig into small pieces.

She turned and walked away, heading for the far side of the clearing. She plunged into the undergrowth, snow dumping onto her back, head and arms. She shook off the deluge and pulled at a tangle of branches. What she came up with wasn't exactly dry, but she supposed it was drier.

Shelby plunged in beside her and began tugging at a branch and biting at the snow. She looked up at Lily, snow crowning her head and back, then shook hard, filling the air around her with a cloud of icy white. Lily laughed. The pup made it impossible to stay in a bad mood.

"What are you doing?" Scott called.

"Getting firewood," she called, and gathered branches into her arms.

She dumped the wood beside Scott. He frowned at her offering. "That doesn't look very dry."

"If you think you can do better, you're welcome to try." She studied the small blaze he had made. If it snowed much harder, the fire didn't stand a chance.

Scott stood. "We need to make a shelter," he said.

"With tree branches?" She pictured the one they had found at the other campsite.

"A snow cave would be warmer." He pulled the collapsible shovel from the back of his pack. "Help me pile up a bunch of snow to work with."

For twenty minutes they shoveled, clearing an eight-foot circle and piling the fresh, wet snow around the perimeter. "That's a good start," Scott said finally. He stuck his shovel in one pile and pulled a multi-tool from his pocket, opened it and folded out a sawtooth blade, then handed it to her, handle first. "See if you can cut some pine branches. We can pile them beneath us to help insulate us from the cold ground."

For the next half hour she sawed away at green pine branches, until her fingers ached and her gloves were sticky with sap. She managed to cut a decent-sized pile of leafy branches, and dragged them back to where Scott was putting the finishing touches on a sort of igloo, with built-up snow sides and tarp-covered branches for a roof. "Get inside and I'll pass the branches to you and you can lay them out on the floor," he said.

Inside, there was scarcely enough room for her to rise up on her knees. When she stretched her arms out, she could almost touch the sides. "Is this going to be big enough?" she asked.

"We'll need to huddle together with the dogs for warmth," he said.

She recognized the logic of what he was saying, but her stomach fluttered nervously. She wasn't worried Scott would try anything...improper. But the thought of being that close to him unnerved her.

"Here. Take this branch."

She took the pine boughs he passed her and spread them on top of the snow floor of their shelter. When she was done, he handed her a second orange tarp. "Lay this over the branches. Do you have an emergency blanket in your pack?"

"Yes." The Mylar blankets were standard first aid supplies.

"Good. We can wrap up in those. Now come out and let's see what we have to eat."

She joined him by the fire as he fed in larger twigs from which he had shaved the bark, revealing mostly dry wood beneath. The blaze wasn't large, but it burned bright and hot. "How did you get the fire going so fast?" she asked.

"Cotton balls soaked in petroleum jelly."

"Huh. I bet you were a Boy Scout."

"Eagle Scout."

"I guess that's where you learned to be so prepared."

"That and the army."

"When were you in the army?"

"Eight year ago." He turned his attention from the fire to his pack. "What have you got in the way of food?"

She opened her pack and pulled out everything she had shoved in there before she left her apartment this morning: protein bars, peanut butter pouches, cheese sticks, nuts, four candy bars, two peanut butter and jelly sandwiches, energy gels, two water bottles, instant hot cocoa mix, and two tiny bottles of peppermint schnapps.

Scott cradled the schnapps in his hand. "What made you bring these?"

"For medicinal purposes."

He laughed—one of the few times she had heard him laugh. It was a nice laugh, deep and rumbling, and it set up a flutter in her chest.

He surveyed the items she had laid out. "You must have been hungry when you packed all this," he said.

"I thought we would be searching again, and when we found Jackson he would be hungry."

He nodded, all mirth gone. "Yeah, he probably is. Though maybe whoever is with him has food."

"We found that candy wrapper," she said. "I hope that means Jackson is eating something."

His own contribution to their stores included chicken bouillon cubes, more protein bars, beef jerky, instant coffee, energy gels, and two ham and cheese sandwiches. "We won't go hungry," she said.

He took out a metal mug, filled it with snow, and set it on a rock beside the fire. "I only have the one cup, but we can share."

He made cocoa and added a slug of the schnapps, then offered the mug to her. The hot, sweet liquid was heavenly, sending a jolt of warmth through her. She refrained from gulping it all and passed it back to him.

They shared the sandwiches and a candy bar each, and a second cup of fortified hot chocolate. By the end of the meal she was drowsy and mostly warm.

The dogs ate jerky and one of the ham sandwiches, and some of the bottled water.

"I feel almost human again," she said as she passed over the empty cup.

"I'm sorry I got you into this situation," Scott said.

The comment surprised her. "I don't think you could have predicted this. And I volunteered to come with you, remember?"

"I should have come by myself. I shouldn't have risked someone else."

"Isn't one of the chief rules for recreating in the wilderness not to go out alone?" she asked.

"I should have gone with my original plan to take Connor."

"Why? Because he's a man?" Her contented mood had vanished, replaced by weary annoyance.

"No. Because he's more experienced."

"What would he have done that I haven't?" she asked. "Except that he would eat more food and take up more room in the snow cave."

He nodded. "You're right. I shouldn't have said that."

She leaned toward him. "What is it about me, exactly, that you don't like?" she asked. "Because if it's just the fact that you didn't personally handpick me for your exclusive team, then you need to get over yourself." She clamped her lips shut. Had she really said that out loud? Maybe the schnapps had been stronger than she anticipated.

He stared at her, his face flushed. This was it. He was

going to fire her, and management would back him up. She'd been out of line—even if what she said was true.

"That's not it at all," he said.

She remained silent, waiting.

He leaned forward, hands gripping his upraised knees. "I didn't want to add you to the avy dog team," he said. "But it had nothing to do with you, personally. I didn't want to add anyone else to the team."

"Why not?"

"Because there are some members of the corporation's board of directors who think the program is too expensive and unnecessary. There's a big push to cut costs these days. It's why Kingdom Mountain was shut down—it wasn't proving profitable enough."

"Kingdom Mountain was at a lower elevation than Sky-Crest," she said. "The season became too short to be profitable."

"Right, but they could have added snowmaking or tried to expand terrain. Instead, they shut it down. Some people at the corporate level are pushing to shut down the avy dog program here, too."

"And one more patroller and dog makes the program that much more expensive," she said. "But if they really want to cut the program, one team more or less isn't going to make that much difference."

He began rubbing Hunter's ears. "I know that. I was just grasping at straws. I didn't mean it personally."

"Instead of keeping this to yourself, you should tell all of us what's going on," she said. "Maybe if we all work together, we can come up with new donors or ways to cut costs or improve our image to the board members."

"I don't like to worry people that their jobs are in jeopardy."

"Except it's the kind of thing we need to know."

He fed another piece of wood to the fire. The temperature had dropped and while the front of her was warm enough, cold seeped through her clothing into her back. Shelby lay on her side between Lily and the fire, snoring softly.

"I hate that a child is in danger," he said. "But if we can find him, it might persuade people who matter that the avy dog program is worth it."

"Do you think Jackson is the one who made that camp we found?" she asked.

"You know him better than I do. Do you think he could have built that shelter and started that fire?"

"He's really smart, but it's hard for me to picture any nine-year-old doing all that. Where would he have gotten the tools, or even the skills to do those things? It's not like his dad is a big outdoorsman, teaching his kid how to survive in the wilderness."

"It definitely looked to me like two people had slept in that shelter," Scott said.

"So Jackson and who else?"

"Another searcher? Everyone in town must know by now that a little boy is missing. Maybe someone decided on their own to go out and look."

"It's strange that you and I didn't see whoever it was," she said.

"Maybe they're trying to remain anonymous."

"They must not have found Jackson," she said. "Or we would have heard." She inched a little closer to the fire and shoved her hands deeper into her pockets. "So maybe what we saw was two completely differently people. Other searchers, or even tourists who don't know about the missing boy. I'm really worried about him. How is he going to survive a second night in this weather, alone? He might have had a few snacks with him, but they would be gone by now."

"Is he the type to panic or give up easily?" Scott asked.

"He's smart and he's quiet. In some ways he's very mature for his age. He's traveled all over the world and is pretty comfortable around all kinds of people. But he's also been very sheltered. Spoiled, even. He's a good kid, but I wouldn't say he's faced much physical hardship."

"Has he done much backcountry skiing? Do you know?"

She shook her head. "I have no idea."

"Why did you leave the job with the Endicotts?" he asked.

"Because Jackson didn't need me. When he turned six he started school full-time."

"What do you do in the summers now?" he asked.

"Different things. Wait tables. Work retail. What about you?"

"I work for the resort," he said. "Maintenance staff. Hunter still gets to come to work with me every day."

"How old is Hunter?" The dog was looking at each of them in turn, having recognized his name.

"He's four. He's been training as an avy dog since he was two months old."

"Same as Shelby."

Shelby gave a single thump of her tail, but didn't raise her head. "So she's about eighteen months old now?" he asked.

"Sixteen. And she's doing great." She dared him to say otherwise.

"What made you want to train an avalanche dog?" He scooped snow into the mug and set it beside the fire to melt.

She could have made up a story about seeing other patrollers work with their dogs, or about coming across the perfect dog to train for the work. Maybe it was the darkness, or the lingering effects of the food and the schnapps, or the novelty of being stranded together, but she decided to opt for the truth. "My brother, Ben, was a ski patroller. He was six years older than me and was training an avy dog, Cache, when he was killed in an avalanche. He was training Cache that day, and was being careful. But a slab of snow let loose and caught him. Friends dug him out, but by the time they found him, it was too late."

"I'm sorry," he said. "That's really tough."

She took a deep breath, steadying herself. "I tried to take over where he left off, training Cache, but I was only seventeen, and I just didn't have the experience, or the time, to do a good job. But I kept the idea in the back of my head. I worked ski patrol for five years before an opening came up in the avalanche dog program at Kingdom Mountain. I applied and was accepted."

"Where did you get Shelby?"

"From a breeder in Steamboat Springs. She comes from a long line of avalanche and search-and-rescue dogs." She reached out to stroke the dog. "My parents helped me buy her. I could never have swung the cost on my own. The resort gave me some money for training, and I scrounged up the rest. But it was worth it. She's been great. Ben would have loved her, too."

"I'm sorry about your brother," he said. "What happened to his dog?"

"Oh, he's living the good life with my parents. He's a pampered senior now. What about you—how did you get into avalanche dogs?"

"Similar story to yours," he said. "My best friend was killed in an avalanche. It took two days to find his body. When I learned that a dog could probably have found him much faster, I wanted to do that for other people—to not make them wait to know what really happened to their loved one. And you always hope that you'll be able to save someone."

"I'm sorry about your friend."

"Yeah." He looked up, snow sifting down onto his cheeks. "He would have loved being out here like this. He would rather be outside in bad weather than cooped up inside almost any time. I try to take comfort in the fact that he died doing something he loved, but I'd rather he was still around."

"How old was he when he died?" she asked.

"He was twenty-six. If he had lived he'd be thirty-three now. A year younger than me."

Ben would be thirty-four if he had lived. The same age as Scott. The two men were nothing alike—except that they both loved dogs and snow.

It was getting colder. She tried to hide her discomfort, but doing a poor job. "You're shivering," Scott said. "Let's turn in. We'll be warmer inside."

"I hope so," she said, and followed him into the snow cave.

She had been nervous about sharing the close quarters, but there was nothing intimate about curling up in a crinkly Mylar blanket while wearing all her clothing. The dogs settled between them. Lily pulled a knit beanie down low over her forehead, gripped the blanket with mittened hands, and waited as warmth gradually seeped into her body and she drifted to sleep.

WHEN SHE WOKE it was still dark. Her whole body ached with cold. Disoriented, she groped beside her, startled to find herself alone. As sleep receded, she sat up and found her headlamp and switched it on. A figure darkened the doorway of the snow cave and she gasped.

"It's just me," Scott said. He crawled past her. The dogs

followed and curled into tight balls, tails over noses. "I'm sorry I woke you," Scott said. "Go back to sleep."

"Yes, sir."

"Sorry. I don't mean to sound bossy."

"I get it. You're used to giving orders."

"I guess that's true." Order or not, she wasn't going to be getting back to sleep anytime soon. Her head ached—probably from a combination of schnapps and not enough water. She found her water bottle, but the contents had frozen.

"Here." Scott passed over his. "You have to keep it tucked in next to your body or it freezes."

She should have thought of that. "Thanks." She drank, greedily, then passed it back.

He drank also. The gesture struck her as intimate, even though he was only being practical.

"I should have asked earlier," he said. "Do you have someone who will be worrying about you—a romantic partner, or your parents?"

"My parents are in Vermont. And I don't have a partner. What about you?"

"My parents are in Utah."

"That must be nice, having them so close."

"I guess. I don't really see them much."

There had to be a whole story there. She was debating whether to ask when he said, "I broke up with my girlfriend four months ago."

His tone of voice made her think the breakup hadn't been his idea. "Rough," she said.

"She said she couldn't see a future with a man who had so little ambition."

"Ouch."

"I get it. Working resort maintenance and ski patrol isn't going to pay for a six-figure lifestyle. For what it's worth, my parents agree with her. They think I'm throwing my life away."

Ouch. "There's something to be said for enjoying the work you do," she said.

"Oh, I think those guys drawing six-figure salaries probably enjoy their jobs, too. I'm just not them."

She understood. The thought of spending every day in an office made her anxious. "Not every woman sees things the way they do," she said.

He didn't answer, except for a soft exhalation of breath that told her he was asleep.

SCOTT WOKE, ON HIS SIDE, his arm draped over someone soft and warm and definitely female. He smiled to himself and moved closer, until he was pressed against her back. She stirred against him, and awareness edged out sleep as he realized this wasn't Madison, his former lover. He froze, and other facts became clear. He and the woman were both wearing a lot of clothing, and lying on the ground.

He sat up and switched on his headlamp. Lily turned onto her back and looked up at him, eyes wide.

"I'm sorry," he said, dread hollowing his chest. "I was asleep. I didn't realize." If she complained to management, he'd be out of a job, the avy dog program ended permanently.

She lay still a moment longer. "It's okay," she said finally, and sat up. She didn't look at him, but didn't seem angry, either. "Where are the dogs?" she asked.

"I don't know. Hunter!"

"Shelby!" she called.

Both dogs came squeezing in, all wagging tails and wiggling bodies. He hugged Hunter to him and buried his face in the dog's thick fur, while Lily did the same to Shelby. "What time is it?" she asked after a bit.

He checked his watch. "Five thirty-two."

She untangled herself from the Mylar blanket and began folding it up. He did the same with his. She left the shelter, Shelby bounding after her. He folded the tarp they had been lying on and by the time he emerged from the snow cave, she was squatting beside the fire, blowing on the tiny flame that licked at a pile of pine needles.

He collected water in the cup he had washed out last night and boiled water for instant coffee. They shared the cup and ate protein bars for breakfast. The dogs ate the last of the jerky.

Afterward, they took down the shelter, scattered the fire and reloaded their packs. At 7:00 a.m. they emerged into open space once more, and he radioed to headquarters. Doug Elam answered. "Scott? You and Lily okay?"

"We're fine," Scott said. "What's the plan for today?"

"I was just talking to the helicopter pilot," Doug said. "They're going to pick you up in…in twenty minutes. Where are you?"

Scott read off the GPS coordinates he had marked. "There's a big clearing here. We shouldn't be too hard to spot."

"Have they heard anything about Jackson?" Lily asked.

"Any sign of Jackson?" Scott asked.

Another long pause. "We haven't found him," Doug said. "But there's been a development."

Doug's voice wasn't reassuring. Scott's gaze met Lily's. She looked as ill as he felt. "What kind of development?" he asked.

"That boy didn't wander out there and get lost," Doug said. "He was taken."

Chapter Seven

The sheriff and Doug were waiting when Lily and Scott and the dogs arrived back at the SkyCrest heliport Monday morning. "What have you heard about Jackson?" Lily demanded as soon as she stepped off the helicopter. "Do you know where he is? Is he safe?"

"Mr. Endicott is meeting us at my office," Doug said, one hand at her back, urging her forward. "We'll know more then."

They piled into a resort SUV, Scott and Lily together in the back seat, the dogs sprawled across their laps. Doug drove, but no one spoke on the short drive to the resort offices. The SUV's heater was pumping out warmth, and Lily found herself drifting off, the exertions of the previous day and her uneasy sleep the night before catching up with her.

She woke abruptly when the SUV parked in the underground garage, and followed the sheriff and the others into the elevator to Doug's office. Denny Endicott met them at the door. His lip had healed and the bruising around his eye had faded to a sickly yellow and brown, but it was the look of hope on his face that was so painful Lily had to look away. "We don't have anything new," the sheriff said.

Denny turned away, but his hunched shoulders and clenched fists were the image of a man fighting to hold himself together. “Mr. Endicott, do you have the note you received?” Sheriff Howard asked.

“Yes. It’s right here.” Denny reached into the pocket of his flannel shirt and took out a plastic bag and passed it over to the sheriff.

“Did it come to you in this bag?” the sheriff asked.

“No,” Denny said. “The envelope was delivered with the day’s mail. I put everything in the bag after I read it. Maybe I didn’t mess up any other prints too much.”

Sheriff Howard lay the bag on Doug’s desk, then pulled on a pair of nitrile gloves and eased an envelope from the bag. “No return address,” he said. “Local postmark. We’ll check with the post office, see if anyone remembers when this came through, but it could have been dropped in a postal box anywhere in the area.” He opened the envelope and removed a single sheet of paper. “Looks like a page torn from a spiral notebook. Lined paper, three-hole punched, no perforations. The message is hand-printed in block letters. ‘We have Jackson safe. Cooperate and he won’t be hurt.’” He looked up at Endicott. “What do they mean—cooperate? What do they want you to do?”

“I don’t know,” Endicott said. “I haven’t heard anything before or since.”

“You never had any previous threats to you or your family, or attempts to extort you in any way?” the sheriff asked.

“None.”

“What about that black eye?” the sheriff asked. “Who gave you that?”

Denny touched one finger to his bruised eye. “I had too much to drink at a client dinner and tripped and fell. It doesn’t have anything to do with Jackson.” He leaned forward, fingers gripping the back of a chair. “We’re always security conscious. We have a good alarm system at home, and I've taught Jackson not to talk to strangers or to go with anyone he doesn't know. I don't understand how this happened."

"Do you have cameras around your house?" the sheriff asked.

"Yes. More than one."

"We're going to want to see all the footage, as far back as you've got. The person or persons responsible for Jackson's kidnapping may have been watching you for a while now."

Endicott straightened. "I thought he was safe here at the resort," he said.

"We've turned over all our surveillance camera footage to the sheriff's department as well," Doug said. "We're also gathering data on every skier whose ticket was scanned yesterday. Something like this never should have happened."

"We've asked for assistance from the Colorado Bureau of Investigation as well," the sheriff said. "We're putting as much manpower as possible on this."

Endicott turned away from them. For the first time, he noticed Lily and Scott on the sofa. "You two were out searching last night, right?" he asked.

Lily took off the knit cap she had been wearing and stood. "Hi, Denny, it's me, Lily Alton."

"Oh, Lily. I'm sorry I didn't recognize you." He swiped a hand over his face. "I'm operating on not much sleep."

"It's okay," she said. His normally full and open face looked thin and drawn, deep lines on either side of his mouth.

Scott rose and came to stand beside her. "We were out searching for Jackson last night," he said. "We followed ski tracks we thought might be his for a long way. He was by himself, and then he wasn't."

"Where did the second set of ski tracks meet up with

him?" Doug asked. He walked to a color map of the resort and the surrounding national forest that took up much of one wall of the office.

Scott and Lily moved to the map, along with the sheriff and Endicott. "Right at this second clump of woods." Scott indicated the spot on the map.

"We found a camp," Lily said. "Where two people spent the night. There was a fire and a shelter."

"Where was this camp?" the sheriff asked.

Scott and Lily studied the map. "About here, do you think?" Lily pointed to a location, and looked to Scott for confirmation.

"Yes, I think that's right." Scott moved his finger a few inches south and west of the spot she indicated. "We spent the night somewhere in here, I think."

"You're sure the camp was recently occupied?" Doug asked.

"Positive," Scott said. "The fire was still smoking."

"There was a shelter there, made of branches and a tarp," Lily said. "I'm sure someone spent the night before last there."

"There were two indentations in the shelter, like two people slept there," Scott said.

"Jackson and the kidnapper," Denny said.

"We don't know that for sure," the sheriff said.

"But who else would be out there in a snowstorm?" Denny asked.

"We followed the tracks as far as we could," Scott said. "Until the snow obliterated them."

"What's out there?" Denny asked. "Where would they be headed?"

"That's all designated wilderness," Doug said. "There aren't any roads." He frowned at the map. "The kidnapper might have arranged for a helicopter to pick them up, but we're not aware of any flights into the area except our own helicopter."

"We'll follow up on that," the sheriff said.

"Someone could have picked them up in a snowmobile," Denny said.

"Maybe," the sheriff said. "But we've been flying drones every time the weather clears enough to allow it and we hadn't seen any tracks."

"Does that mean they're still out there?" Endicott asked. "Jackson must be exhausted."

"They could be heading for Pandora," Scott said.

"Where's Pandora?" Denny asked.

"It's a ghost town on the other side of this ridge of mountains." The sheriff indicated a jagged ridge near the top of the map. "But you'd have to be crazy to try to make it all the way there on skis, especially with a kid in tow."

"Crazy or desperate," Denny said.

"If you received that letter today, wouldn't it have had to be posted by Saturday or earlier?" Scott asked.

Endicott looked to the sheriff. "I would think so," he said. "Don't you, Sheriff?"

"The stamp is canceled," the sheriff said. "According to the postmark, it was mailed Friday."

"That's taking a big risk, isn't it?" Lily asked. "What if their plan failed and they weren't able to grab Jackson? What if the weather didn't cooperate?"

"Or what if the letter was lost?" Scott asked. "Why not just send an email or a text, or make a phone call or hand-deliver a note?"

"The Endicotts' security may have scared them away from the house," the sheriff said. "And the kidnapper may not have been tech-savvy enough to send an electronic message without us being able to trace it."

"If the kidnapping didn't happen, it would be easy to dismiss the letter as a crank message," Doug said. "Mr. Endicott might have even thrown it away without reporting it to the sheriff."

Denny nodded. "I might have."

"We think it likely there are a group of individuals involved," the sheriff said. "We'll get a team to Pandora and see if we can intercept them. We'll also continue to fly surveillance in the area."

"What can we do to help?" Scott asked.

"Go home and get some rest," the sheriff said. "We'll take it from here."

"Thank you for your help," Doug said. "You can go now."

Reluctantly, Lily followed Scott and the dogs out of the room. She waited until they were in the elevator headed to the ground floor before she spoke. "I notice no one offered us a ride home," she said.

"I'll take you," he said.

He led her to the motorcycle, parked in a back corner of the parking garage. This time, Shelby didn't hesitate to hop into the sidecar. Lily was able to fasten her helmet without help, and the ride to her apartment—in the daylight this time—wasn't as unnerving. Scott drove slowly, and she clung to him, as much for the bodily warmth as to steady herself. The clock tower in the middle of the ski village indicated it was almost noon. Crowds of skiers convened in the cobblestoned courtyard that fronted many of the restaurants and shops. People in brightly colored pants and jackets lounged on benches or carried skis and snowboards toward the lifts. Children laughed and dogs barked. Shelby's ears were straight up, but she maintained discipline—or maybe she was too frightened to risk leaping from the moving vehicle. Scott guided the bike between pedestrians and parked cars, and turned onto the main road leading away from the village.

Minutes later, he turned into the apartment complex. “Thanks,” she said again, after he had parked and she had returned his helmet. “I guess I’ll see you tomorrow.”

“Let me know if you hear any news about Jackson,” he said.

“Yeah. You, too.” She waved, then turned and followed Shelby into the building.

She waited inside, out of sight, and listened to the roar of the motorcycle recede as he headed toward his own building. The complex had an elevator, but it was primarily used for freight. Lily always used the stairs, considering the climb part of her exercise routine. Even weary as she was, it didn’t feel right to resort to the elevator, so she started up the stairs.

Shelby bounded up ahead of her, still full of puppy energy.

Inside, she fed and watered the dog first. She debated making tea, but decided on the shower first. The hot water elicited a blissful groan as it sluiced over her. For the first time in almost two days she began to feel truly warm. Lavender-scented steam surrounded her, and she fought the urge to lean against the tile wall and fall asleep standing up.

Her intention was to make tea, eat something, then go to bed. But instead of feeling sleepy, after she ate she had the jangly, electrified feeling of having been awake too long to relax. Her mind replayed the events of the previous two days like a poorly plotted movie. Jackson had been so happy when she had spoken to him two days ago. How could he have just…disappeared? The thought of him in the wilderness somewhere, with a stranger or strangers, cold and frightened and maybe even hurt, tore at her.

She powered up her laptop and searched until she found a map similar to the one on Doug's office wall. From what she had seen yesterday and this morning, the wilderness area was rugged, the direct route to anywhere interrupted by dense woods, imposing ridges or deep ravines. Reaching Pandora would mean a traverse of a pair of rocky mountain ridges full of dangerous obstacles obscured by snow, steep drop-offs, the near-constant threat of avalanches, and bitter winds. How was a child supposed to survive all of that?

She stared at the map until her vision blurred, and was about to close the screen when another thought occurred to her. If going over the mountain to reach Pandora was so difficult, was it possible to go *around*? She traced a Forest Service road that led from town, skirting the wilderness area and ending a couple of miles before Pandora. The kidnapper would have to be careful to keep himself and Jackson out of sight, and the journey to get to the road from the place where they had spent the night would require navigating around dense woodlands and uneven terrain. But that route would also afford more places to hide or seek shelter from the weather.

She punched in the number for the sheriff's office. When a woman answered, Lily identified herself, explained that she had been part of the search for Jackson and asked to speak to the sheriff. The woman transferred the call, but the person who answered wasn't the sheriff. "Sheriff Howard is very busy right now," the man said. "I'll be sure he gets your message."

"Who am I speaking to?" she asked.

"I'm one of the deputies. That's really all you need to know."

That was not all she needed to know, but weariness was stealing over her once more. "This is Lily Alton," she said. "I was with the sheriff earlier today. Tell him that I think instead of traveling over the mountain, Jackson's kidnapper might try to go around. It would be safer, and they'd have more places to hide."

"That's an interesting theory," the deputy said. "But I don't think you're right."

"Just tell the sheriff what I said and let him decide," she said.

"Thanks for calling," the deputy said, and hung up.

She stared at the phone, shaking with anger. She scrolled and found Scott's number. Wait until he heard about this. But she hesitated with her finger over the number. Scott was exhausted. He was probably already asleep. He wouldn't welcome her calling and waking him up to complain about a dismissive deputy.

She set down the phone. As much as she wanted to help Jackson, there really wasn't anything she could do right now. All she could do was rest up and be ready if she was needed. And wait.

Chapter Eight

On Tuesday Lily and Shelby went back to their regular post with Ski Patrol. Scott and the rest of the group were there, and everything at the resort was running normally. "I don't have an update on Jackson Endicott," Scott told them at the beginning of the patrol meeting.

"News reports said he'd been kidnapped," Brian said. "His family received a ransom note or something."

"I heard the family was contacted," Scott said. "I don't know if there was a ransom request or not." He consulted the clipboard in his hand. "Law enforcement is dealing with that. We need to focus on our work here. I need a dog and handler to talk about safety to the ski school kids at ten a.m. Lily, can you take that?"

"Sure." She sat up a little straighter. "Shelby loves kids."

"We've got a set of posters you can use for your presentation," Scott said. "Just go through those and you should be good."

He moved on to patrol assignments, then dismissed them. She waited until everyone else had left before she approached Scott. "You really haven't heard anything about Jackson?" she asked.

He slotted the clipboard onto a shelf in the ski patrol office. "They're more likely to tell you news than me. After all, you know the family."

"I've thought about calling Denny and asking, but I hate to bother him." She nibbled her thumbnail. "I'm so worried about Jackson."

"We all are, but there's nothing we can do. Let's just get on with our work." He opened a file drawer and took out a large envelope. "Here are the posters for the safety talk. You'll be talking to the second- and third-grade kids. I think there's two classes. Meet them midway down Easy Street at ten o'clock."

At ten, she skied up to a group of ski school children waiting at the edge of the trees, midway down a beginner's run. Shelby, newly released from her kennel and sporting a new baby-blue SkyCrest bandanna, danced with excitement as they approached the children. "Patroller Lily is here to talk to us about ski safety," Kristen Waters, one of the instructors, introduced her.

"Hey, everybody," Lily said. "This is avalanche dog Shelby. She's going to help me with today's presentation."

"Can we pet her?" a little girl in a pink snowsuit and helmet asked.

"You can all pet her after the talk," Lily said. "First, I want you all to listen carefully. At the end I'm going to ask some questions and if you answer a question correctly, I have prizes." She held up the stickers and trading cards she had brought along to hand out to them.

The posters featured cartoons of the SkyCrest mascot, a baby-blue dinosaur named Shred, demonstrating lift etiquette, the importance of respecting other skiers and other tips for safe skiing. Lily enlisted Shelby to demonstrate points such as taking turns, and looking up the slope before you merged on a new trail. "What happens if you don't stay still on the chairlift?" Lily asked.

"You can fall off," a little boy in a helmet with flames painted on the side said.

"That's right." Lily looked at Shelby. "Show them how you fall, Shelby."

Shelby dramatically plopped onto her side in the snow, sending the children into fits of giggles.

"You get a prize for answering my question," Lily said. The boy chose a sticker.

"I want a trading card!"

"I want a sticker." Other children clamored for the prizes.

Lily asked more questions about the material they had just covered and handed out stickers and cards to all the children. Every one of the children was so adorable, she thought. Some of them weren't much younger than Jackson. "Do any of you know Jackson Endicott?" she asked as a little girl deliberated over her choice of prize.

"I heard about him on the news last night," one boy, the tallest of the group said. "But I didn't know him."

"What happened to him?" a little girl asked.

"He disappeared," the boy said.

"I'm sure they're going to find him very soon," Kristen said. She sent Lily a warning look.

"Hey everybody, you've been such a great group," Lily said. "If you take your skis off, you can come pet Shelby."

"Why do we have to take off our skis?" a girl asked.

"Ski edges are very sharp," Lily said. "They can cut a dog's paws and hurt them very badly. So never ski close to a dog."

The kids raced to kick off their skis, then descended on the dog, who greeted them with a wagging tail. Lily moved over to Kristen. "Sorry I mentioned Jackson," Lily said. "I didn't mean to upset anyone."

"It's okay," Kristen said. "What a terrible thing to happen. I'm afraid to let any of these kids out of my sight now."

"Have you seen anyone hanging around the children?" Lily asked. "Watching them or anything?" Though the note Denton Endicott had received seemed to indicate that Jackson was the deliberate target, maybe the kidnapper had looked for him first among the other kids at the resort.

Kristen shook her head. "I haven't seen anyone. And we do watch for things like that. Anyone hanging around the kids who we don't know for sure is a parent gets reported to security."

"How often do you have to report someone?" Lily asked.

"Not often, but even once is too much."

Lily was packing up the posters and preparing to call the kids off Shelby when a familiar figure in a black helmet skied up. Scott nodded to her. "Don't let me interrupt."

"I was just finished."

"Is everybody ready for lunch?" Kristen called.

"Yes!" The children scrambled to line up.

"Shelby, come!" Lily called.

The dog loped over to her side, while the ski school students returned to their skis. "Did you need me for something?" she asked Scott.

"What were you and Kristen talking about?" Scott asked.

She frowned. Why did he care about that? "I asked her if she had seen anyone suspicious hanging around the kids," she said. "I thought maybe whoever took Jackson might have looked for him with other children."

"It's not your job to investigate this," he said.

"I happen to think it's every person's job to look out for

kids," she said. "A little boy's life is at stake, and I'll do anything I can to help."

She braced herself for an angry reaction, but he appeared unfazed. He watched the ski school class head down the hill, an undulating line following their instructor. "You're really good with the kids," he said. "I bet you were a good nanny."

Was he complimenting her, or insinuating she should leave patrol and go back to taking care of children? She wished he wasn't so hard to read. "I try to do my best at every job," she said. "Whether that's changing diapers or training an avalanche search dog."

He was still watching the retreating children. "I've been thinking a lot about Jackson."

"I have, too," she said. "I looked at a map again last night, and I don't think the kidnapper would try to go directly over the ridge to Pandora."

He turned to look at her, though she couldn't see his eyes clearly through the amber goggles he wore. "Why do you say that?"

"Going over the ridge is the shortest route, but it's also really risky and really hard. It would be a lot easier to go around the mountain."

"A lot farther, too."

"Yes, but safer."

"Maybe you should talk to the sheriff about your idea."

"I tried calling and leaving a message last night. The deputy who took my call was pretty dismissive."

"I've been thinking about going over to Pandora myself and looking around," he said.

"Could you even get there?" she asked. "I mean, don't you think the place is crawling with law enforcement?"

"I don't know. But it's worth checking out, I think."

"When would you go?"

"It's my regular day off tomorrow," he said. "If I get an

early start I can get there and back in no time. If you drive up Matlock Road there's a trail at the end that goes right into the wilderness area."

"Can you make it up there on a motorcycle this time of year?"

"Probably. From there it's probably only a couple hours' hike to Pandora."

"You shouldn't go by yourself," she said.

"I'd have Hunter with me."

"Is Hunter Lassie now? Does he know how to go for help?"

The corners of his mouth twitched, almost as if he was holding back laughter. "I thought maybe you'd like to go with me."

"I'm on the schedule for tomorrow."

"Anders wants next Sunday off. You could switch with him."

Her heart jumped. "Then yes, I'll go with you."

"You sure? You don't want to think about it?"

"I told you, I want to help Jackson."

"Good." He paused, then added, "Let's take your car. That way we'll for sure get to the trailhead. I'll be at your place tomorrow morning at six." Without waiting for more, he planted a pole and skied away. She watched him go, struck once more by how much he stood out among the crowds of skiers—tall and graceful, but skiing with purpose. A man on a mission, even if the mission was to get to the bottom of the mountain. His suggestion to look for Jackson on their own had surprised her. One more bit of proof that he didn't always play strictly by the rules.

DARKNESS STILL PAINTED the world in shades of gray as Scott stood beside his motorcycle waiting for Lily to emerge from her apartment. She had texted she would be out in five minutes. He stamped his feet and watched his breath fog the air. The thermometer at his apartment had registered minus nine degrees Fahrenheit when he left.

A sharp bark from Hunter alerted him to Lily and Shelby's approach. Shelby shot toward them and tackled Hunter. The two dogs rolled on the snowy pavement then leaped up, tails waving.

"Good morning," Lily said. "My car is over here." She led the way two rows over to a blue Subaru Outback, and stood on tiptoe to heft her skis into the rack on the car's roof. Scott followed and added his own skis, then they shoved packs, boots and poles in to the back of the vehicle. "Do you have your beacon?" he asked.

"Yes. And it's fully charged."

"Just checking."

She grinned. Was she amused at his inability to stop being the boss? Or because he was so predictable she had anticipated what he would say?

She pulled an insulated mug from the side of her pack, slid the top open and sipped. The tantalizing aroma of cinnamon filled the air.

"What are you drinking?" he asked.

"Black tea with cinnamon and cloves." She tilted her head and considered him. "Let me guess—you drink black coffee."

She wasn't wrong. "Let's go," he said.

She slid into the driver's seat and buckled her safety belt. Shelby arranged herself on the back seat next to Hunter. "Have you heard anything from the sheriff?" she asked as he settled into the passenger seat.

"No. I called Doug last night and he said a couple of

agents from the Colorado Bureau of Investigation interviewed him, but they wouldn't say anything about the case."

She started the car and backed out of her parking space. "I called the Endicott house last night," she said. "The man who answered said they weren't taking calls and there was no news. I didn't recognize his voice, so I thought maybe he was a cop."

"We may get to Pandora and find the place crawling with cops," Scott said.

"What are we going to tell them if they ask what we're doing?" She turned onto the road that led to the back country.

"We tell them we came to ski," he said. "Plead ignorance."

She chuckled softly.

"What's so funny?" he asked.

"You don't look that clueless."

"What do you mean?"

"Everything about your screams 'competent and informed.' I mean that as a compliment, but no cop is going to believe you live in a cave and haven't heard a thing about a boy being kidnapped. You can't help looking like you know exactly what you're doing."

"Then I've fooled you," he said. "I have no idea if we'll find Jackson or not, but I have a hard time sitting around doing nothing."

"Then you and Shelby have a lot in common."

There she went, making him the butt of a joke again. "I'm glad you find me so entertaining," he said.

"Would you rather I be intimidated?" She sipped her tea.

"I'm not trying to intimidate anyone."

"When I first started work here, you were pretty forbidding," she said. "Until I figured you out."

"Oh, you figured me out, did you?" Whereas she confounded him more every minute.

"You're like a lot of guys I've met—cool and detached on the outside, but inside you care deeply about things. I think it frustrates you when other people don't care as much, like with the avalanche dog program."

The assessment hit him like a punch in the gut—he didn't like being so transparent. "Were you a psychology major?" he asked.

"No, but I pay attention to people." Another sip of tea. "It's my superpower."

"Too bad your superpower can't tell us what happened to Jackson."

She sighed. "Yeah. Too bad."

They both grew quiet, though he was aware of her, only a few inches away, focused on her driving. He had seldom been around someone so self-contained, content with silence.

She turned the car onto the snow-packed Forest Service road that led to the trail they wanted. "Have you been here before?" he asked.

"No. I looked up the directions last night online. And I read about Pandora. Apparently, it used to be a gold mining town."

"Right. There are half a dozen log buildings still standing, some of them in pretty good shape. It's a popular destination for hikers in the summer, and there are a few more modern summer cabins near the town site that are still kept up, but hardly anyone comes up here in winter, except occasional cross-country skiers."

At the end of the road, she parked at a locked gate. "It looks like a lot of people were parked here recently," she said, pointing to the packed snow on either side of the road.

They let the dogs out to run around while they collected their gear. They both donned packs, boots and skis. "It's about two hours, maybe a little less, to Pandora from here," he said.

"Should we turn on our beacons?" she asked.

"Not yet. We have to go a ways before needing to worry about avalanche danger." He took a pistol from his pack and slid it into the pocket of his jacket. She watched him, eyes wide. "We don't know what we might be up against here, or who we might run into," he said. "I want to be ready."

"Okay." He couldn't read the emotion behind that single word.

"I was military police," he added.

"Ah. That explains a lot."

It explained the gun, maybe. He wasn't sure what else she meant, and he hesitated to ask. No doubt she would have an interesting explanation, but he wasn't ready for more dissecting of his character right now. "Come on."

They squeezed around the gate and set out skiing side by side down the closed roadway. Dark green firs and the bare white trunks of aspen thickly lined the road on either side. They had been skiing about fifteen minutes when the road curved and the woods opened onto a view across a meadow up against the mountains. Rosy light bathed the snow-filled meadow in a pink glow and painted the mountain peaks in gold. Lily stopped and stared, her lips parted.

He skied up beside her. "What is it?" he asked. "What do you see?"

She turned toward him. She hadn't lowered her goggles yet, and her eyes were damp. "It's so beautiful," she said.

She was beautiful, her face flushed from exertion and cold, lips so soft and inviting. Had he ever felt as awed as she looked now?

He forced his gaze away. "It's too cold to stand around," he said, and skied off.

She caught up with him, and they skied hard for the next mile, the dogs running ahead, then falling back to lope along in their tracks. After another half hour, they stopped and put on their avalanche beacons. They left the trees behind and steadily climbed, the only sound the squeak of their skis on the snow and their own labored breathing.

The sun was climbing overhead before they came to a wooden signpost that directed them to Pandora. The town itself was tucked into an open flat, or park, between two peaks. The buildings sat in the shadow of the mountains, snow piled halfway up the sides of most of the structures. The largest building, a former dormitory for miners, was missing half its roof and leaned precariously to one side, but several of the smaller structures—mine offices and miners' homes—appeared intact except for a few broken windows.

"Why isn't there anyone here?" Lily asked. She turned to him. "The sheriff's deputies should be here, and Colorado Bureau of Investigation people. This should have been the first place they came."

"Maybe they were here and left when they didn't find anyone," he said.

She turned to study the scene again. "I don't see any tracks. It doesn't look like anyone has been here since it snowed on Sunday."

"Maybe this elevation got more snow last night," he said.

She moved forward on skis, sliding right up to the front of the closest building. She leaned forward to peer into the window.

"See anything?" he called.

She shook her head. "And I don't smell smoke. If someone was sheltering here, they'd have to build a fire, wouldn't they, as cold as it's been at night."

It was still cold. Well below freezing, he guessed. The arctic chill stung his bare cheeks and had him tucking his gloved fingers into his jacket to try to thaw them.

They skied all the way around the ruins, but found nothing but a set of fox tracks and the smaller imprints of rodents.

"How did people ever live up here in the winter?" she asked when they were back at the entrance to the town. She glanced at the steep slopes on three sides. "Weren't they worried about avalanches?"

"Avalanches are what finally drove people to abandon the town," he said. "For a while I think they worked the mines in summer only, but then the gold played out completely. Everyone left shortly after the turn of the twentieth century."

She hugged her arms across her chest and rubbed her shoulders. "It's creepy."

"Maybe we should go back," he said. Initially, he had planned to ski past the town, maybe even over the ridge above. They might spot Jackson or his kidnapper. But looking up that steep slope, with its heavy blanket of snow, sent danger warnings through him. Steep slopes and fresh, heavy snow were prime conditions for an avalanche. He wouldn't risk his life—much less Lily's—on such a reckless foray.

"I'm ready to get out of here," she said, and turned toward the trail back to her car.

The return trip took less time. They were traveling downhill and said little. As she was unlocking the car, Scott's phone rang. He waited until they were inside, engine on and heater running, before he looked at the missed call. "I've got a message from Doug Elam," he said. "I'd better see what he wants."

He called his voicemail. Doug's Georgia drawl was thick with agitation. "If you get this in the next five minutes, I need you and Hunter to the staging area below Axis Ridge. We've got a big slide, two people potentially involved."

Chapter Nine

"Two people? Do they think Jackson and his kidnapper were caught in the avalanche?" Lily asked, the words coming out as fast as the hammering of her heart.

"Doug didn't say." Scott studied his phone for a moment longer, then tossed it on the dash. "There's a Forest Service road that cuts across to the base of the ridge," he said. "I'll tell you where to turn."

"Shelby and I are only certified for inbound searches," she said, and felt foolish as soon as the words were out of her mouth. Scott knew this—and it wasn't as if she didn't want to help.

"Just do what I tell you," he said. "It'll be fine."

She turned the car around and headed back the way they had come. She drove as fast as she dared on the narrow, snow-packed road, teeth clenched, gripping the steering wheel so hard her fingers ached. She lost traction on every curve, and fought to bring the fishtailing car back under control. Scott gripped the dash with one hand and said nothing.

Phrases from her training played in her head. *A person caught in an avalanche has a 92 percent chance of surviving if they are rescued within fifteen minutes. Survival rates drop by 3 percent for every additional minute someone is buried.* Those were just one set of statistics. A Canadian study put the survival rate at 86 percent after ten minutes and only 10 percent after thirty-five minutes. The whole point of training dogs was to get to victims as quickly as possible, increasing their chances of surviving.

She had been so focused on training Shelby to locate someone quickly that she hadn't thought about how long it could take to reach the site of a slide to even begin the search.

She pressed down harder on the accelerator and thought of Jackson. *Hang on*, she silently told him. *Please hang on.*

They reached the cutoff road and followed the ruts left by other vehicles to where the track abruptly ended at a six-foot berm of packed snow. Half a dozen vehicles were parked haphazardly in front of the berm. Lily fit the Subaru in between a Jeep and a lifted 4X4 pickup and cut the engine. Scott retrieved his phone and checked the screen. "Twenty minutes," he said.

She followed him to the back of the Subaru and retrieved her pack. "Put your beacon in receive mode," he said.

She did so. "What about Shelby?" she asked. The dog had her head over the back of the seat and was whining softly.

"She can search with Hunter," Scott said.

The dogs raced ahead of them, to the group standing at the edge of the snowfield. The jagged tops of trees jutted through boulder-sized clumps of snow that marked the path of the snow slide, pine needles scattered across the surface like confetti. Dirt, broken branches and boulders littered an area as wide as a football field.

Some people were already searching, moving in a line across the snow, pausing every step to plunge long, flexible poles into the snow. They were feeling for anything soft enough to be human.

Adam Derocher from C-RAD jogged over to them. "A

helicopter searching for the boy who went missing from SkyCrest saw the slide run and called it in at 11:56," he said.

Lily did the math—twenty-seven minutes had passed since that call. "The spotter saw two people skinning up the ridge just before the snow turned loose," Adam continued. "He didn't have anywhere to land."

"Where were these two people?" Scott asked.

"On the east side." Adam pointed. "I want the dogs to search over there."

Like Scott, Adam knew Shelby was only certified to search inbounds, but he apparently wasn't going to pass up the chance to use her now that she was on the scene. Both dogs were eager to go. Hunter had done this before, and was communicating his excitement to Shelby, who raced between him and Lily. Shelby had been part of dozens of training exercises by now, and she knew searching meant a reward of playing with her favorite toy. But she had only found volunteers hiding in man-made snow caves, never anyone buried by an actual avalanche.

Tugging on Shelby's lead, Lily followed Scott and Hunter across the snowfield, stumbling over blocks of compacted snow, dodging chunks of rock and broken trees, then sinking to her knees in an unexpected drift. By the time Scott halted at the far edge of the field, she was breathless, one knee throbbing where she had twisted it.

"I'm going to release Hunter first," Scott said. "After he takes off, let Shelby go and give her search command."

Hunter sat, trembling with anticipation, his attention fixated on Scott. Scott unclipped the dog's lead. "Hunter, find!" he commanded, and Hunter took off, nose to the ground.

"Shelby!" Lily had to repeat the dog's name twice before Shelby focused on her. She removed the leash. "Go find!" she said.

Shelby took off in Hunter's wake, head down and moving back and forth, casting for scent.

Less than three minutes later, Hunter gave one sharp bark and sat, gaze fixed on a patch of snow. "He's found something!" Scott shouted, and raced toward his dog.

Lily followed. She dug at the compacted snow with her hands while Scott used the folding shovel from his pack. Hunter dug, too, sending plumes of snow flying between his legs. Other searchers joined in.

"I've got a leg," someone shouted, and the searchers shifted their efforts to several feet above this location, hoping to uncover the person's head.

Five frantic minutes later someone uncovered hair, and then the whole face and upper torso. The man's skin was blue, his lips frozen in a grimace, his head at an unnatural angle. Adam knelt beside the body and felt for a pulse, then shook his head. "He's gone," he said. "Looks like his neck was broken."

Lily looked away. The body in the snow didn't even look real, but was still shocking. Scott led Hunter away. He praised the dog and offered the rope toy that was his reward for a successful find, but the dog knew something wasn't right and kept looking back toward the unknown man's icy grave.

While the others worked to free the rest of the body, Lucy looked around for her dog. "Shelby!" she shouted, hands cupped to her face. "Shelby, come!"

Finally, she spotted the dog at the very edge of the snowfield, pawing at something. Lily made her way to the dog, who by this time had a piece of blue fabric in her mouth. "What have you got?" Lily asked.

She wrested the cloth away from the dog and was examining it when Scott and Hunter joined them. "What is it?" Scott asked.

"It looks like blue nylon," she said. "Is it part of a jacket?" Jackson had been wearing a blue jacket, she remembered that.

Scott examined the scrap of fabric, which was about as big as his gloved hand. "Maybe it's part of a backpack," he said.

Both dogs had returned to the spot and were worrying at something. Scott and Lily shoved them out of the way and began digging. Within minutes, they had unearthed a small backpack with an internal hydration bladder—a style favored by skiers and snowboarders. Lily stared at the battered pack and tried to remember what Jackson had been wearing when she had spoken to him on Saturday.

"There's a name on the inside flap," Scott said. He turned the pack around so he could read the name written in black marker, but fell silent.

"What does it say?" Lily demanded.

He met her gaze, looking every bit as hollowed-out as she felt. "It's Jackson Endicott."

THE VOLUNTEERS PROBED and dug in the compacted snow for the next two hours and found no sign of Jackson, or of anyone else. Denton Endicott arrived, along with the sheriff, and they stood over the pack, Endicott's normally ruddy face slack and devoid of color. "Jackson got that pack for Christmas," he said. "I'm the one who wrote his name in it." He bowed his head, jaw clenched, but after a moment he looked up at the snow spread out like a rumpled blanket. "How could the pack be here and you haven't found my boy?"

"Avalanches have tremendous power," Adam said. "They can tear the clothes from a man."

Avalanches could also break bones and crush skulls. Scott had seen bodies recovered that looked practically untouched, while others were battered almost beyond recognition.

The sheriff put a hand to Endicott's back. "I need you to look at the man we found and see if you recognize him," he said.

Scott followed the two men, wanting to hear what they would say. He had taken Hunter back to the truck an hour before, the dog exhausted from repeated fruitless searches. Lily and Shelby had disappeared in the mass of volunteers. He needed to find her soon, but for now he stuck close to the sheriff and Endicott.

The man's body had been placed on a litter and covered with a blanket, then slid into the back of one of the two ambulances that waited on scene. The driver opened the doors and stood aside to allow the sheriff and Endicott to lean in. Scott waited to one side. He'd gotten a good look at the body earlier—a fit white male in his mid- to late thirties, clean-shaven with light brown hair and brown eyes, dressed in good-quality but not top-of-the-line ski gear. "I don't recognize him," Endicott said after a moment. "But he looks so ordinary. Not the kind of guy to stand out."

"No," the sheriff said. "Apparently, there's no identification on him. Maybe we'll get lucky when we take his fingerprints. We found these things with him." He moved to a tarp on the ground nearby and pulled it aside to reveal a large backpack. "It looks like he was prepared to survive out here for some time. There's a lot of food and cold weather gear in there."

"Maybe he came out here to search for Jackson," Endicott said.

"Then why not have ID with him?" the sheriff asked.

"There was also this." He pulled an evidence bag from inside his parka and showed it to Endicott. Inside was a handgun.

Endicott face went even paler. "My poor boy," he whispered.

"You're sure you've never seen the dead man before?" the sheriff asked.

Endicott shook his head. "Never."

They retreated from the ambulance. Suddenly, Endicott turned to Scott. "Are you the one who found him?" he asked. "You and your dog?"

"Yes, sir."

"And you found Jackson's pack?"

"Lily and Shelby found that," he said.

"Then why haven't you found Jackson? What do you think happened to him?"

"I don't know, sir. If he was buried very deeply, that can make things more difficult."

"How long has it been since the avalanche?" Endicott asked.

"Almost three hours," Scott said.

"Then if Jackson is under there, he's dead," Endicott said.

Scott said nothing.

"Don't try to shield me," Endicott said. "If Jackson was buried and you haven't found him by now, he's dead, isn't he?"

Scott nodded. "I'm sorry," he whispered.

Endicott stared out across the snow again, blinking rapidly. "We might not find him until spring," he muttered.

"We're going to bring heavy equipment out here to dig starting tomorrow," the sheriff said. "We need to uncover all the evidence we can, and if your boy is here, we'll find him."

The sheriff led Endicott away. Scott started toward the parking area, then stopped and scanned the scene for Lily and Shelby. Lines of volunteers continued to probe the snow, but Adam had agreed there was no need to exhaust the dogs further, now that the chance of finding anyone alive was virtually zero. Yet there were Lily and Shelby, on the far side of the slide, the dog's plumed tail waving like a signal flag.

Scott trudged over to them. "What do you think you're doing?" he demanded. "Are you trying to kill your dog?"

She stared at him, wide-eyed. "I've been trying to get Shelby to come back to the car for the last hour," she said. "But she keeps searching this same section of the slide. She actually tried to lead me into the woods three times, but when I follow her, she loses the trail after about a dozen yards."

"You're the one in charge, not your dog."

"But why is she acting this way?" Lily asked. "She's never done anything like this before."

"She's frustrated because she didn't find a person, only a pack. And it's obvious to anyone she's exhausted."

Shelby lay on the snow, tongue lolling, though her head remained up, ears alert.

Lily shifted the leash to her other hand. "Come on, girl," she said. "We have to call it a day."

The dog rose, but looked back toward the edge of the snowfield, not moving. "Come!" Lily commanded.

Shelby's ears twitched, but she didn't move, not even when Lily yanked on her leash. Clearly, Lily hadn't taught the dog who was in charge. "You're wasting my time," Scott said, and bent and scooped the dog up. Then he stalked back across the snow, Lily trailing behind him.

The dog was small for a Malinois, but she still weighed at least fifty pounds. Scott, worn out from the day's activities, struggled to carry her over the rough terrain. "Put her down," Lily said. "I can carry her."

Scott could hardly manage. There was no way Lily, who looked ready to drop where she stood, was going to be able to carry the dog. As for Shelby, she had become an inert mass in Scott's arms, like a dog cast in lead.

When they exited the avalanche field he did set the dog down. Lily grabbed the leash and stalked ahead, pulling the dog after her. She might be tired, but clearly she was angry, too. She was waiting beside the car when he reached it. "I would never do anything to harm my dog," she said.

"I don't believe you would, intentionally," he said. "But the thing about dogs is that they are so devoted and tenacious that they will literally work until they drop. It's up to us to see that that doesn't happen."

She loaded Shelby into the car, then slid into the driver's seat. "I'm sorry," she said as she started the engine. "I was too focused on finding Jackson, and not enough on Shelby. I won't let that happen again."

He nodded and fastened his seat belt. She backed the car out of the parking spot. "Nobody feels good about days like today," he said.

"How could we find Jackson's pack and not find Jackson?" she asked. "If he was skinning up that ridge, he would have had it on."

"Maybe he stopped to get something out of it and took it off right before the slide triggered," Scott said. He could picture it. Skinning was hard work. Maybe Jackson wanted to shed a layer of clothing, or put away his gloves, or check the water level in his hydration bladder. "When the slide released, it would have been torn from his hand."

"Then where is Jackson?"

"He could be anywhere in that debris field," Scott said. "Under feet of snow."

"What if he's not there?" she asked. "What if he got

pushed out of the way to the side? That's why I kept following Shelby into the woods. I thought Jackson might have run in that direction."

"If that happened, why didn't he come back when he saw all the searchers?" Scott asked. "Even if he didn't know his kidnapper was dead, he should have known there were people in that crowd who would help him."

"I don't know," she said. "And I don't know why Shelby lost the scent trail every time after only a few feet."

She stared straight ahead, and he wondered if she was crying. "I'm sorry about Jackson," he said. "Knowing him the way you do makes this harder."

She sniffed, but still didn't look at him.

"I saw his father a few minutes before I found you," he said. "He identified the pack as Jackson's. He said he didn't recognize the man. The sheriff said he hopes they can match the man's fingerprints to a known person."

"The sheriff said they're bringing heavy equipment out to dig tomorrow. They're looking for more evidence. Maybe he means the pack."

"Maybe they'll find Jackson's body," she said. "As awful as that is for his family, not knowing for sure what happened to him must be worse."

When they reached the townhomes where they both lived, Lily had to wake Shelby to get her out of the back seat. "Oh honey, I'm sorry." Lily knelt and hugged the dog. "I shouldn't have let you work so long."

"She'll be okay," Scott said. "She's young, and she doesn't appear to be limping."

She kept her cheek pressed to the dog's fur, not looking at him. "You're not going to kick me out of the avy dog program because of this, are you?"

"No! What made you think that?"

"You were so furious with me. And I understand why. A big part of our training is protecting our dogs, and I wasn't doing that."

"We all make mistakes," he said. "The lessons we learn by screwing up are the ones that really stick." He hadn't been wrong to correct her, though maybe he could have been gentler. The anguish he had heard behind her question made him feel like the worst kind of heel. "I know I wasn't exactly welcoming, but I'm glad you're in the program. And you and Shelby did a good job today. She found Jackson's pack."

"I wish she had found Jackson."

"We all wish that." He patted her shoulder. She looked up at him, and his gaze shifted to her lips. She appeared delicate, but he had seen how strong she could be. Her lips were soft like her, but they would be strong, too. Expressive. Communicating what they wanted.

He took a step back. "Good night." Without waiting for a reply, he turned and hurried off toward his apartment. He was Lily's supervisor. He had no business kissing her, especially when she was exhausted and vulnerable.

He prided himself on always doing the right thing. But why was the right thing so hard this time?

Chapter Ten

Scott slept fitfully, reliving the afternoon's search for Jackson Endicott over and over again. Then the search for Jackson morphed into the search for Clark—the frantic probing and digging, the desperate effort to cling to hope, the surrender to despair. And then the waiting and not knowing, trying not to think about the suffering Clark might have endured in his last moments, and everything Scott might have done to save his friend.

He rose early Thursday and tried to banish the nightmares with a shower and hot coffee, but the gray mood clung to him like a second skin as he rode into the silent ski village just as the sun rose. On his way to the ski patrol office he saw the light was on in Doug's office. He detoured there and found the resort director behind his desk, looking like a Ralph Lauren ad, in a Nordic sweater and dark jeans, the scent of some expensive cologne hovering around him. He looked up when Scott tapped on the door. "Come in, Scott," Doug said. "What can you tell me about the avalanche yesterday?"

Scott sank into a chair in front of Doug's desk. "Hunter found a body. Maybe the kidnapper."

"Alleged kidnapper," Doug said. "They still haven't identified him. And we don't know for sure he was the person who took Jackson."

"You sound like a lawyer," Scott said.

"Only a man who was married to one. Do you want coffee?"

Scott shook his head. "Have you heard anything else from the sheriff? Besides the fact that they don't have an identity for the dead man?"

"I had to meet them here at six a.m. so they could collect every recording from every camera in the resort," Doug said. "They're looking for images of the man."

"I thought they already looked at the footage," Scott said.

"Not everything. And when they viewed the video before, they were focused on Jackson and anyone he might have talked to. This time they have a specific face they're trying to find."

"Too bad finding him doesn't help us locate Jackson."

"The sheriff said it's pretty certain the kid's dead," Doug said.

Scott winced. "We found his backpack. At the edge of the avalanche field. Until we find a body, we won't know for sure what happened to him."

"You think there's a chance he escaped? Where did he go?"

"I don't know. And he's probably dead." He didn't like saying it, but there was no sense ignoring harsh reality.

"They're still conducting air searches," Doug said.

"They are?"

"One flight a day. But until they have a clue where to look, that's a shot in the dark. An expensive one. If the kid's last name wasn't Endicott, I doubt they'd be doing that."

"Lily and I skied over to Pandora yesterday," he said.

"No one was there. It didn't look like anyone had been there since the first snow."

"You and Lily Alton?"

"She was Jackson's nanny. He'd be more likely to come to her than a stranger."

"Guess so. Was there something in particular you needed to see me about this morning?"

"No." Scott shoved to his feet. "I just wanted to know if you'd heard anything about Jackson."

"I'll let you know if I do."

From Doug's office, he made his way to ski patrol headquarters. Lily was waiting at the door, Shelby at her side. "You're early," he said as he unlocked the door.

"Only by a few minutes," she said. She moved quickly past him into the office, but not before he saw the shadows beneath her eyes. She was probably as exhausted as he was. He was tempted to tell her to take a sick day and go home, but he couldn't play favorites. She would probably resent the suggestion, anyway.

Over the next quarter of an hour, the rest of the team reported in. They fed the dogs, gathered their gear and assembled for the morning meeting. With light snow overnight, they had some routine avalanche mitigation to do, targeting the areas most likely to be unstable. "We need to plan on a delayed opening for Lifts 11 and 12," Scott said. "After all the lifts are running, we need to reposition the pads on the lift towers for Lift 6. And the snow fence is down in part of the mid-mountain terrain park, so Raz, you and Trey take care of that."

He read off each team member's duties for the day, then dismissed them. As Lily gathered her gear, Scott found her. "How are you feeling this morning?" he asked.

She stowed a water bottle in her pack and zipped it shut. “I’m fine.”

“How is Shelby?”

“She’s fine, too. We both crashed after we got home yesterday.”

“I’m sorry if I was too hard on you yesterday,” he said.

She finally looked at him, clearly surprised. “You weren’t. You were right. If I’m going to do this work, I need to protect Shelby, even when she won’t protect herself.” She leaned closer, her voice a little softer. “Are you okay?”

“I’m fine.”

“I was remembering what you told me, about your friend. The one who was killed in an avalanche. You must think of him every time you’re called out to search.”

“Yeah. I do.” He had to force the words out over the sudden constriction in his throat. “But you probably think about your brother.”

“Yes…but I don’t think it’s the same for me. I wasn’t with him when he died. I wasn’t there for the search, either. It was only after I started training with Shelby that I even thought about it much.”

“I don’t think these searches are easy on anyone. Maybe that’s something we need to stress more in training—the emotional toll this can take.”

She shrugged on her pack, then donned her helmet. “We’ll get through it,” she said, and left.

He followed her out the door a few moments later and spotted her standing with Denny Endicott. “Scott!” she called, and waved him over.

He jogged over to them. “Everything okay?” he asked, looking from her to Endicott. The grieving father didn’t look any better than he had the day before, his skin pale, eyes hollow. "Do you know where I can find Doug?" Endicott asked. "He isn't in his office."

"I can see if I can raise him on the radio." Scott unclipped the radio from his pack. "What do you need?"

"I got another message this morning. From the kidnapper. They say they still have Jackson. They say I have to cooperate if I want to see my son again."

TEN MINUTES LATER, Lily stood with Scott and Denny in Doug Elam's office. Doug had summoned the sheriff, but he wasn't waiting to question Endicott. "What do they mean, cooperate?" he asked. "What do they want you to do?"

"I don't know. Someone called right after I received the note and said there would be more instructions later." He looked down at the note that lay on the corner of Doug's desk. Like the first, it was written on plain paper, and Denny had placed it into a clear plastic bag. "I asked to speak to Jackson, to prove he really is alive, but they wouldn't let me."

"If they say they have him, that must mean he's alive," Lily said.

"It could be a hoax."

She winced at Scott's words. Maybe he was right, but did he have to dash Denny's hopes so plainly?

"That's why I asked for proof that Jackson is okay," Denny said. "I want to believe he's alive, but after yesterday..." His voice trailed away.

The door opened and Sheriff Howard entered, accompanied by the undersheriff, Tricia Dees. "What's this about another note?" the sheriff asked.

Denny showed him the note and told him about the phone call that had followed. "If they won't give me proof Jackson is alive, does that mean he really is dead?" he asked.

"Mr. Endicott, you must know the odds of your son having escaped that avalanche yesterday afternoon were slim to none," the sheriff said. "I'm sorry, but I won't lie to you."

Denny nodded.

"I think this is a desperate attempt by the kidnappers to get what they want, even though they know they've lost Jackson," Howard said.

"Have you been able to identify the man who was killed yesterday?" Denny asked.

"Not yet," the sheriff said.

"What about the excavation at the avalanche site?" Denny asked. "Has that started?"

The sheriff looked as if his shoes were pinching his feet. "We've run into a snag there. The avalanche occurred in a designated wilderness area. The Forest Service doesn't want heavy equipment in there tearing things up."

"We're trying to get a special permit," Tricia said.

"So far, no one's budging," the sheriff added.

"What else are you doing to find my son?" Denny asked.

"We're reviewing footage of all the video at the resort," Howard said. "We're trying to find the man whose body we recovered. We hope that will help identify him or find his connection to Jackson. We're still interviewing people who were at the resort that day and might have seen Jackson with someone. We've sent the man's fingerprints and image to the CBI and the FBI for help in identifying him. We're analyzing records for any similar crimes. We've put the word out to the public, asking anyone with information to contact us. We have Jackson's picture on social and traditional media."

"But you're not physically searching for Jackson," Denny said. "Why not?"

Lily was thankful she wasn't facing the hard look Denny gave the sheriff, but the lawman didn't wilt. "We're a small department, assisted by two agents from the Colorado Bureau of Investigation. We're doing everything we can, but we don't have the manpower to continue a ground search. We have to focus our resources on where we have the chance of getting the best results."

He didn't say *we can't waste our time looking for a body*, but Lily thought that was probably what he meant.

Denny's expression hardened. "I'm going to use every resource at *my* disposal to find out what happened to my son," he said, then left the room.

Doug was the first to break the silence that blanketed them after Endicott's departure. "I think we all need to get back to work," he said.

"Come on," Scott said, and headed for the door.

Lily followed. She caught up with Scott at the elevator. "Do you really think Jackson is dead?" she asked.

The look he sent her stung—a mixture of pity and impatience. "You know the statistics about surviving an avalanche. I'm sorry, but that boy is buried under feet of snow right now."

She bowed her head, not wanting him to see the disbelief in her eyes. He would think she was foolish. Everyone else clearly thought Jackson was dead, killed by that wall of snow that had broken away from the ridge yesterday afternoon. Everything in Lily's training told her that, too, but she couldn't give up. Not on the boy she had fed and bathed and played with from the time he was a toddler. Jackson wasn't any missing child. He was part of her. And she couldn't give up on him, no matter how foolish that might seem to some.

SCOTT LOOKED FOR Lily at the end of the day. Not finding Jackson had hit her hard, and he wanted to make sure she wasn't blaming herself for what had happened. Shelby wasn't in her kennel at patrol headquarters, so that probably meant Lily had taken the dog out for some exercise. He released Hunter from his kennel as well. They could help sweep the runs for any stragglers and look for Lily and Shelby at the same time.

He spotted Connor as he exited the lift office and flagged him down. "Have you seen Lily and Shelby?" Scott asked.

"I saw them headed up Lift 4 a few minutes ago," Connor said. "I was just headed up 2 to start sweeping Buttermilk Basin."

"Good," Scott said. "I'll see if I can catch up with Lily and we'll head down the front side." This section of beginner and easy intermediate runs was often the last of the day to clear of eager skiers hoping to get in one final run.

The last few skiers were boarding Lift 4 when Scott and Hunter arrived. The liftie, a lanky blond from New Zealand, grinned as the pair approached. "How's it going, mate?" he asked.

"We're doing okay, Noah," Scott said as he looked back at the approaching chair. "How are you?"

"Can't complain, though I wouldn't mind a sweet pup like this one." He leaned over to pat Hunter.

"Did Lily and Shelby ride up ahead of us?" Scott asked.

"Sure did. Shelby batted those big brown eyes at me like the flirt she is." He leaned over to boost the dog into the lift chair. "Have a good run, mate."

As they rode the lift up, Scott scanned the terrain below for Lily and her dog. The crowds were thinning, the sun low in the sky and temperatures cooler. He made note of the need to reposition the snow fence that marked the beginning of the terrain park. A snow dump had partially obscured a couple of trail signs. They'd need to check those first thing tomorrow. Snow was in the forecast tonight. They'd need to set charges to clear the slopes above Tessa's Trees and the Glades.

At the top of the lift, Hunter bounded off and Scott skied out after him. "Have you seen Lily and Shelby?" he asked the liftie, a tall woman name Gigi.

"They headed down May Day about ten minutes ago," she said.

May Day was a wide blue run that opened to views of the distant snowcapped peaks. Two-thirds of the way to the bottom, he spotted Lily and Shelby, surrounded by half a dozen preteens. Hunter let out a bark and raced to join them, but Scott called the dog back. He stopped a few feet upslope and ordered Hunter to sit. Lily was running Shelby through a bunch of basic obedience exercises—sit, stay, roll over—to the delight of the children. Scott watched for a while. She had pushed her goggles up on top of her helmet and was smiling at the children, who cast adoring glances at her and the dog. Wisps of light brown hair had escaped from the helmet and framed her face, and her cheeks were flushed pink from the cold. Most of the time, he avoided looking at her directly, but now, with all her focus on the dog and the children, he felt free to do so. Her beauty hit him like a kick in the gut, leaving him breathless and staggered. He'd felt it the very first time he laid eyes on her, and recognized the danger in the feeling. He was her boss. He wasn't supposed to feel this way about her. Or at least, he wasn't supposed to act on his feelings. And he wouldn't. He respected her, admired her even, though her presence on the team made him uncomfortable. That was his problem, not hers.

She looked up, and for a fraction of a second their gazes locked. Another kick in the gut. Her smile had vanished, and she quickly looked away. Yeah, she definitely didn't feel the same attraction he did.

"I have to go now, kids," she said.

"No!"

"Show us one more trick!"

"Please!"

Smiling, she shook her head and called Shelby to her side. She lowered her goggles and gripped her poles.

"Is that your boyfriend?" a girl with brown braids and braces asked.

Lily glanced at Scott again. "No, it's my boss." She turned from the children and skied over to join him. "Did you need something?" she asked.

"How are you doing?" he asked.

"I'm fine."

Her tone was brusque, and she didn't look at him. "What did you need to see me about?"

I needed to make sure you were okay. But he couldn't say that. "I need to get a copy of Shelby's certification for our files."

Her head snapped up. "You're worried about that *now*?"

He had been trying to come up with something innocuous when the words popped out. He looked away, face burning. "Just get it to me whenever you get a chance."

She shook her head. "I can't really think about that right now."

He started to walk away, but that was the coward's path. Instead, he faced her. "What's wrong?" he asked.

She didn't answer.

"Is it Jackson?" he asked. "It's natural you're upset about him. It's always harder when you know the victim."

"Don't say that word."

"What word?"

She grimaced. "Victim."

"Lily." He tried to make his voice gentle. "You know the odds of Jackson still being alive are slim to none."

"You don't know that." He couldn't see her eyes behind the reflective goggles, but he was sure she was glaring at him. "His backpack was found at the edge of the avalanche field. Jackson could have been thrown free. He could have skied out of the path of the avalanche. He could be out there alone in the woods, without his pack." Her voice broke, and she pressed her lips together.

He wanted to pull her close and comfort her. To hold her and tell her he understood her grief. He had lost people he cared about before. He knew that feeling of helplessness, of not being able to do anything to bring them back.

But of course, he couldn't do that. "I know it's hard," he said. "But you can't beat yourself up like this."

"You're not listening!" Her voice rang in the stillness. They were alone on the run now, the shadows from the tall trees alongside the run stretching out to embrace them. "As long as there's a chance he's alive, we should look for him," she said. "That's our job, isn't it—to rescue people? Not to leave a child to freeze to death in the woods." Her voice shook, and her bottom lip trembled.

"Lily…"

She turned and drove one ski pole into the snow and sped away. Shelby barked and raced after her.

Scott let her go. He wouldn't get through to her now. She would have to come to terms with the situation by herself. She was right. They were supposed to help people.

He hated that he couldn't do anything to help her.

Chapter Eleven

Icy wind froze the tears that streamed from her eyes as Lily raced, blindly, down the slope. Thankfully, there were no guests left for her to collide with. At the bottom of the run, she stopped and tried to clear her vision. Shelby sat at her feet and looked up, whining, the picture of distress.

"Oh, girl, it's okay." Lily sniffed, then bent and hugged the dog. She glanced back to see if Scott had followed her, but the run was empty. Good. She didn't want to hear any more of his talk of "victims" and "accepting the situation."

She hurried to headquarters, collected her belongings and headed for the shuttle stop.

But when she got off at her apartment, she didn't go inside. Instead, she climbed into her car and drove to the Endicott home. The gates at the end of the long driveway were closed, but she pressed the intercom. "This is Lily Alton," she said. "I really need to see Denny."

"Lily?" a man's deep voice asked.

"Is that you, Mike?"

"Denton isn't seeing anyone right now, Lily," Mike said.

"Please," she said. "I need to talk to him about Jackson."

A long pause. Had Mike gone to consult Denny? She wondered if she should press the intercom button again, but then the gate began to swing open. "Come on up," Mike said.

Mike was waiting in the doorway as she mounted the steps, Shelby beside her. He didn't say anything, merely held the door open wider, then shut it when they were all inside. "How is Denny?" Lily asked.

"About as wrecked as you would expect," Mike said. "But he said he wanted to see you."

She followed him toward the back of the house, to Denny's home office. Mike knocked, then opened the door and held it for her.

Denny rose from the sofa and came to meet her, taking both her hands in his. "It's good to see you, Lily," he said.

She nodded, her throat too tight to speak. Denton Endicott looked beaten and deflated. Deep bags under his bloodshot eyes spoke of sleepless nights, and his shoulders sagged as if bearing the weight of the world. He glanced behind her at Mike. "You can leave us, Mike. Thanks."

When they were alone, he returned to the sofa. "Come sit with me," he said.

She sat, and Shelby lay on the floor between them. Denny rubbed the dog's ears. "Thank you for looking for Jackson," he said.

"I want to do anything I can to help."

She waited, thinking he might have questions about what had happened. But he fell silent, his hand stroking the dog's head, over and over. Shelby sat, eyes closed, clearly enjoying the attention.

After a long while, Lily cleared her throat. "I wanted to talk to you about Jackson," she said.

He nodded. "You were one of his favorite people," he said. "He told me all about how you were training Shelby to be an avalanche rescue dog."

"Jackson is a great kid." She refused to speak of him in the past tense. "So smart, and interested in so many things."

"He's a smart kid," Denny said. "Quiet, but he's always thinking."

"Do you remember when he was five years old and figured out how to reprogram the sprinkler system to flood the yard at night?" she asked.

Denny smiled. "He thought it would freeze overnight and make an ice rink. I had to explain it wasn't cold enough yet."

"I've been wondering about some things," she said. "How did the kidnapper know Jackson was going to be at the resort that day?"

"I've wondered that, too," he said. "But Jackson would have told anyone who asked that he planned to go skiing. Or maybe whoever it was had been there every Saturday, just waiting for him to show up."

"But why kidnap Jackson? Did the kidnapper ask for ransom?"

He hesitated, then said, "Not money."

"Something else?"

He looked away and blew out a breath. "You can't tell anyone," he said. "No one knows this."

She waited, afraid to speak. Denny shoved to his feet and began to pace. "Did you know my company has contracts with the federal government?"

She shook her head. "No."

"It's not all of our business, but it's an important segment. Most of the stuff we do is for the United States military, and it's all top secret." He raked a hand through his thinning hair. "Right now, we're developing a new guidance system for weapons. State-of-the-art stuff."

"I'm not sure I understand what this has to do with Jackson's kidnapping."

"These people who have contacted me want the plans for that guidance system."

"Did you tell the police that?"

"No."

At her surprised look, he turned on her. "The system is top secret. Everyone who works on it has a top security clearance. I took an oath that I wouldn't share the information with anyone. I can't risk some loose-lipped clerk in the sheriff's department sharing this information with the media or someone who turns out to be a Russian spy."

He spoke with such fervor she shivered. But on the other hand, this sounded almost cartoonish—Russian spies? Here in the mountains of Colorado? "Is that who you think is behind this?" she asked. "Russians?"

"I have no idea. Certainly all of the people on my team are Americans."

"How many people know about this system?" she asked.

"Only the team working on the project. They're all sworn to secrecy, but it's possible one of them let something slip. People talk."

"I think you should at least tell the sheriff," she said.

"I don't have a lot of faith in that lot," he said. "They think everything is over now that Jackson is…now that he's gone."

"But something like this—wouldn't the FBI get involved?"

"Maybe. I haven't decided if I want that, either."

"Is that how you ended up with a black eye and a split lip the week before Jackson was taken?" she asked. "Because someone was trying to intimidate you?"

He slumped into his chair once more. "I guess no one really believes I was that clumsy," he said. "Yes. A couple of thugs waylaid me after my meeting that night. They told me I had to leave the information they wanted in a drop box the next day. If I didn't, they would kill me."

"But you didn't do that?"

"No. I won't betray my country that way."

Even now, battered and grieving, his voice was full of conviction. "Did you tell anyone about this—the sheriff or someone else?" she asked.

"No. I didn't think they'd take me seriously. I didn't really believe the threats, either. Not at first." He buried his head in his hands.

"Do you have any idea who is doing this?" she asked.

He lifted his head. "I can't think it could be anyone who works for me," he said. "Most of them have been with me for years. But maybe one of them said something to a friend or relative who's not as trustworthy."

"What about Preston Smith?" she asked. "He's a new employee, isn't he?"

Denny sat up straight again. "Mike told me Preston came by the house that night and upset you. But I don't think Preston would do anything like this. He has an impeccable résumé and is excellent at his job. He passed the background check and received his security clearance with no problems at all. And he's reported for work every day since Jackson went missing and doesn't act any differently."

"Maybe he's part of a group of people. I mean, if we're talking foreign governments and spies, maybe they recruited a bunch of different people to work for them." Wasn't that how it worked in movies? She reached out and touched the back of his hand. "Maybe you should contact the FBI."

He sighed. "You're right. I… I just can't think with Jackson gone. I don't care about anything else."

"Had Jackson had much experience out-of-doors?" she

asked, remembering the questions Scott had asked her. "Besides skiing at the resort, I mean."

"I'd taken him fishing a few times. Hiking in the summer. Why do you ask?"

"I was thinking. If Jackson was kidnapped, he would be the type to try to get away, don't you think? I mean, he'd try to figure out a plan that would let him get away."

"Probably. But he couldn't have counted on an avalanche."

"What if he did?" She leaned toward him, hands on her knees. "What if he set that avalanche on purpose?"

"How would he do that?"

"If he had read much at all about avalanches, he could have been familiar with the kinds of conditions that make them more likely—steep, exposed slopes, especially if they're south-facing. Windblown slopes or cornices. He would have known that skiing across such terrain could trigger a slide."

He looked dismayed. "Are you saying Jackson caused his own death?"

"No! No!"

"Then what are you saying?"

"I don't want to give you false hope. And I may be completely wrong. But the place where we found Jackson's backpack—that was on the edge of the snowfield. And there was no sign of Jackson."

"Adam said the backpack was probably torn from his body."

"Maybe. But the straps on the backpack weren't ripped. It looked to me more like someone took it off and set it down and it was caught up in the avalanche."

"What are you saying?"

She sat up straighter and took a deep breath. "I'm wondering if Jackson got away. Maybe he fled his kidnapper. He shed the backpack so that he could travel faster, and as a distraction. The kidnapper would see the backpack and stop to investigate. But what if in pursuing Jackson, the kidnapper triggered the avalanche? He was caught in the slide, but Jackson was far enough ahead to get away."

"Do you really think that's what happened?"

"I don't know. Maybe everyone else is right and Jackson was killed in the avalanche. But I think it's possible."

"Adam Derocher said we might not find his body until spring."

"In the meantime, what's the harm in looking for him outside the avalanche?" she asked.

Denny's gaze remain fixed on her. "The sheriff says he doesn't have the resources."

"I want your permission to look for Jackson—me and Shelby." At the sound of her name, the dog's ears pricked.

"You don't need my permission for that."

"I don't want to do it without your knowledge," she said.

"Do you need money? Supplies?"

"No. Just your permission."

"It might not be safe," he said. "I don't know the people I'm dealing with on this, but they could very well be from a foreign government, or aligned with one."

"I'm just a skier with a dog. They won't be looking for me."

He considered this for a moment, then nodded. "All right. Are you sure there isn't anything I can give you to help?"

She thought for a moment. "Do you have a satellite phone?"

"I can get one."

"It would be good to have. Cell phone coverage isn't very good out there."

"Do you need anything else?"

"Maybe some of Jackson's warmest clothes? If I find him, he'll need them."

He nodded again. "When do you want to start?"

"In the morning. First light."

"What about your job?"

"I'll call in sick. My boss knows I'm upset about Jackson. I'll tell him I'm not doing well and I need time." Scott would probably be relieved to hear she planned to stay home. "Or I'll just find someone to trade shifts. We do that all the time." It would be better if she didn't have to talk to Scott.

Denny stood, and she rose also. "Be back here first thing in the morning," he said. "I'll have the phone and the clothing for you."

WHEN SKI PATROL members gathered the next morning, Scott surveyed the group. Brian and Anders were there with their dogs, along with Renee Castro, Chase Sergeant, Livi "Raz" Rasmussen, and Carson Slade. "Where's Lily?" he asked, a knot of worry already forming in his chest.

"She called early this morning and asked if I would switch with her." Nina spoke up from a back corner.

Scott checked his clipboard. Sure enough, Nina wasn't on the schedule. "Is Lily sick?" he asked.

"I don't think so," Nina said. "She just said she had something to do."

Scott nodded and forced himself to move on to the day's assignments. But when the meeting was over, he waylaid Nina. "What did Lily say, exactly?" he asked.

She frowned. "What I told you—she said she had something to do today and asked if I would trade with her. She's going to work next Saturday for me."

"Did she sound upset about anything?"

"No. I don't know. It was six in the morning. I wasn't exactly awake."

"She didn't say anything about me?"

Nina's eyes widened. "Why? What did you do?"

What had he done? Not been sensitive enough? Pushed her too hard? "She was just a little upset when I left her yesterday."

"She knew that kid who was kidnapped and ended up dying in that avalanche, right?"

"Who told you that?" he asked.

"Lily told me she knew the kid," Nina said.

"I mean, who told you he died?" Scott asked.

"It's all over the news this morning." Nina pulled out her phone and showed him. A headline declared Son of Endicott Industries Owner Killed in Avalanche.

Right. So Scott wasn't the only one who made the logical assumption that Jackson Endicott had been killed in that avalanche. But Lily couldn't accept that. She was such a kind and caring person. Of course it hurt her to think of a child killed, especially one she knew.

"She probably just needed a day to get her head together," Nina said. "You're not going to give her a hard time about it, are you?"

"No. Of course not."

Nina looked doubtful, but said nothing.

Scott headed out toward the helicopter pad to help with the morning's avalanche control. But all day as he worked his thoughts kept returning to Lily. He made the last sweep of the day down May Day, and the memory of her and Shelby entertaining the children the day before pained him. He had handled the whole situation with her and Jackson so badly.

He loaded Hunter into the motorcycle's sidecar and headed home, but instead of parking in his usual spot, he drove around to Lily's side of the apartments. He needed to apologize—to make her understand he hadn't meant to be so rough on her. "Come on Hunter," he told the dog. "Let's go see Lily and Shelby."

Chapter Twelve

Friday morning, Lily and Shelby slogged through the snow-choked forest between the avalanche site and Pandora. They had been out here for hours and made little progress. At six thirty that morning she had met Denny at a side door of his home. Like a spy passing on top secret documents, he had handed over the satellite phone and a fresh set of clothing for Jackson. "Let me know the minute you find anything," he said.

"I will," she said, as she stowed the items in her backpack. "But I may not find anything."

He nodded. "I didn't tell anyone what you're doing."

"No sense embarrassing us both if this turns out to be for nothing." She slipped the backpack onto her shoulders.

"It's not that." He glanced around. They were alone, standing in the light from a single fixture over this side door, darkness surrounding them. Their breath hung in clouds between them, and biting cold seeped beneath her coat collar. "I've been thinking a lot about our conversation last night—about who could be behind this," he said. "I'll admit I made a mistake, not taking this threat seriously. I think someone on my team has to be involved in this, and I'm going to ask the FBI to take a closer look at Preston Smith."

"That's a good idea," she said. "The FBI is bound to have resources the local cops don't."

"But this kidnapping," he said. "It's so personal. So close to home. It makes me wonder if someone in my own household might be involved."

Her heart jumped. "Do you really think so? Why would anyone who knows Jackson put him in danger?"

"I don't know. But what you said—about someone knowing Jackson was going to be at the ski resort that day—it got me thinking. Maybe the kidnapper was guessing—but what if someone here told them about our plans?" He shook his head. "I just don't want to take a chance."

"Yeah. I guess that's smart." She shifted her feet, trying to fight off the cold. "I'll let you know what I find, either way." She turned away.

"Lily?"

She paused to look back. "Yes?"

"Be careful."

She liked to think she was always careful. That was one reason it had taken most of the day to get even this far in her search. She had parked her car a little after seven, tucking it into the trees down the road from the area that had been cleared for parking. First, she had to skirt the avalanche area itself. At that early hour, no one was around, though the evidence of the previous day's work was scattered across the snowfield. Long avalanche probes stuck up from the ground like the stems of dandelions whose heads had been scattered by heedless children. In places the snow had begun to melt, exposing the jagged chunks of trees and dirt-spotted boulders.

She and Shelby stopped at the place where they had found Jackson's pack. Shelby sniffed around, but alerted on nothing. The dog wasn't trained to search for anything other than people buried in snow, but Lily decided it wouldn't hurt to try her out. She pointed toward the woods and gave the command, "Go find."

Shelby tilted her head in a questioning look, then put her nose to the ground and moved into the trees.

Five yards in, the trees were so thick it was difficult to maneuver. Thick white aspen trunks stuck up like pickets, and the fallen remains of older trees were hidden beneath the snow, dangerous traps for a skier. Lily finally took off her skis and her pack. She strapped the skis to her pack, then shimmied sideways through the tree trunks. Was this why Jackson had removed his pack? It would certainly have made fleeing through the woods faster.

She tried calling for him. "Jackson! It's me, Lily!" But the trees and snow swallowed up her words. Jackson would have to be standing very close for him to hear her.

Shelby climbed over yet another fallen tree and came to stand beside her, tongue lolling. Scott's words, berating her for wearing the dog out, came back to her. She slipped off the pack and took out a bottle of water and a foldable bowl. "I know this is tough," she told the dog. "You're doing great." She checked the dog's paws for any cuts or signs of frostbite, but all looked well.

She set down the bowl, and Shelby drank. Lily took a few swallows of water from the bottle, then stowed it and the bowl. She checked the GPS on her phone. They were traveling in the right direction to reach Pandora, but was this the way Jackson had come? He might have tried to head back toward the ski resort. Or he might be wandering lost in the woods.

Or he might be dead. If he hadn't been killed in the avalanche, would he have frozen to death overnight? He didn't have his pack with him, which meant no extra clothing, food or water. His dad said he had spent a little time in the outdoors, but would he know how to seek shelter or start a fire?

The thought of finding Jackson dead made her wish she wasn't out here alone. Over the years it had been drilled into her how risky it could be to ski or hike or climb solo. But what choice had she had? No one else believed Jackson had survived the avalanche.

She checked her phone. Ordinarily about this time she would be skiing the runs at the resort, on the lookout for anyone in trouble. She might take Shelby out for a run and visit some ski school classes, or even help ferry an injured skier to the clinic at the base of the runs.

Had Scott been angry that she had traded shifts with Nina without checking with him first? Maybe *angry* was too strong a word, but he had probably been annoyed. He always wanted everything to be perfect and orderly under his command. Too bad he was overseeing ordinary people and not robots. People were messy a lot of the time.

Shelby pawed at Lily's leg, bringing her out of her reverie. "Come on," she told the dog. "We have to keep searching." She couldn't give up on Jackson yet.

No one answered Scott's knock on Lily's apartment door shortly after four thirty Friday afternoon. He had tried texting, then calling, but she wasn't answering. Was she that upset with him? He pounded on the door again, harder this time.

The door of the apartment next to Lily's opened. A scowling man leaned out. "She's not home," he said.

Scott stepped back and sized up the man. Mid-forties, bags under his eyes, in need of a shave. "Do you know where she went?" he asked.

"She and her dog left early this morning. I was heading

out to for my shift driving a county plow just as she was coming out. She works ski patrol."

"Right. But she wasn't at work today. I'm her boss."

"Huh." Bushy eyebrows drew together in a sharp vee. "She had her skis and pack and the dog and everything, all loaded into her car. I don't know where she was heading."

Her car. But she usually took the shuttle to work. "Thanks." He turned to leave.

"I hope she's okay," the man called after him. "She's a sweet girl. Great dog, too."

Scott returned to his motorcycle, but stopped beside it to survey the cars in the lot. Lily's Outback wasn't there—so where was she?

She had called Nina at six this morning, and said she had "something she had to take care of." Then she had left here with her skis, gear and dog. She was worried about Jackson. She thought he was still alive, alone in the wilderness.

A cold knot formed in his stomach. She had gone to search for Jackson—he was sure of it. She had gone by herself, not telling anyone where she was headed. It broke every rule of wilderness safety.

But understanding softened the edge of his anger. Lily had gone out because she cared. He hadn't let himself believe her conviction that Jackson was still alive, so she hadn't been able to turn to him for help. Maybe his dismissal of her concerns had kept her from confiding in anyone else. She probably felt she had no choice but to conduct a search on her own.

Hunter hopped into the sidecar, and Scott mounted the motorcycle and started it. "We're not headed home just yet," Scott said, and patted the dog's neck. The first thing he had to do was find some transportation that wasn't a motorcycle. He'd never make it where he needed to go on the bike.

He pulled out his phone and scrolled through his contacts, then selected a name. "Hey, Brian, it's Scott. I need a favor."

"Sure, Scott." The easygoing patroller and his golden retriever, Daisy, had similar sunny attitudes, though both were good at their jobs.

"I need to borrow your truck," Scott said. "Maybe overnight. Something's come up and the motorcycle isn't going to cut it traveling any distance in this weather."

"Sure. You can use my truck. Is everything all right? Anything I can do?"

"Thanks. I really appreciate it. Could I come get it now?"

"Sure."

Scott ended the call before Brian could ask for more details. He started the motorcycle and rode the few miles to Brian's duplex. He exchanged his bike keys for the truck keys, loaded up Hunter, then headed back to his apartment, where he collected skis, avalanche beacon, and a pack full of food, water and emergency gear. He had enough supplies to at least get him to Lily and bring her to safety.

All he had to do now was find her.

He drove to the avalanche site. Long shadows stretched over the snowfield, darker pools where people had been digging, lighter shades where the snow was still untouched. The cleared-out space where rescue vehicles had parked was empty. He drove slowly past the lot, back onto the road. She wouldn't have wanted to leave her car where it would stand out. So she would have left it nearby, but not in an obvious place.

He found it a few hundred feet from the parking area, a blue Subaru Outback snugged up against a tall pine. He was sure this was Lily's car.

Scott parked the truck next to the Outback, let Hunter out, then began unloading his gear. He shoved extra supplies in his pack and called for the dog. The big Lab was sniffing all around the Subaru, tail wagging. "Do you smell Lily and Shelby?" Scott asked.

He walked over and peered through the windows of the Subaru. Nothing to see. Of more interest were the ski tracks leading away from the vehicle. He followed the tracks along the edge of the avalanche field, to the place where they had discovered Jackson's pack. He spotted tracks of a dog, headed into the woods, the ski tracks alongside them.

He wasn't a trained tracker, but it didn't take an expert to identify the place where Lily had removed her skis. The terrain was too crowded with obstacles to make skiing safe, which was why he had left his own skis behind at the truck. He continued on foot, sinking to his knees in softer snow only occasionally, following Lily's and Shelby's tracks. A few feet into the woods, the shadows deepened. Cold crowded around him. He shoved his goggles on top of his helmet and donned a head lamp. "Lily!" he shouted. "Shelby!"

He stepped into a hole, lost his balance and ended up sprawled in the snow. He lay there for a moment, trying to catch his breath. Hunter bounded over and nudged at him, whining.

"I'm okay." He shoved onto his knees, then stood. Now he was the one being foolish, stumbling around in the dark. He should go home. If Lily hadn't returned to her apartment by morning, he could call the sheriff.

But the thought of leaving her out here alone, in the cold, tore at him. He cupped his gloved hands to either side of his mouth. "Lily!" he shouted again.

Hunter barked, then bounded away. "Hunter! Come back here!" Scott stumbled after the dog. "Where are you going?"

Then Scott saw the light—a small bluish moon bobbing through the trees in the shrouded darkness.

Hunter barked again, and raced toward the light.

"Over here!" a woman called. "I've found something!"

LILY HAD SPOTTED the shoe print half an hour before, just when she was about to turn around and make her way back to her car. It was the clear impression of a single ski boot, but boy-sized, about twelve inches long. Just the one clear print in a line of trampled snow, as if someone had traveled this way.

She followed that trail of disturbed snow, Shelby right in front of her. The dog began to whine. "Do you smell Jackson?" Lily asked.

Heart in her throat, she tried to move faster. The narrow beam of the light from her headlamp allowed her to avoid the largest obstacles in her path, but outside of that light was a black void.

Shelby barked again, then whirled and barreled past Lily, almost knocking her over.

"Shelby!" Lily shouted, but the dog paid no attention.

Lily peered ahead, trying to determine what had made the dog change direction so suddenly. Was there a big animal up ahead—a mountain lion?

In the distance, another dog barked. Not Shelby. Lily turned to look behind her again. Shelby barked in answer, then Lily heard someone calling her name.

Relief surged through her. She wasn't going to have to do this alone. "Over here!" she shouted. "I've found something."

She told herself she should have been surprised to see Scott moving toward her, but she wasn't. He knew her feelings about Jackson's possible fate, and he was just stubborn enough to venture out in the darkness to look for her.

He arrived just behind the two excited dogs—red-faced and scowling. "What are you doing out here by yourself?" he growled.

"I think you already know the answer to that question," she said. She dipped her head to illuminate the path at their feet. "I've been following this trail. I think it's Jackson's."

His frown didn't fade. "This trail could have been made by anything. You could be following an elk, or even a moose."

"Earlier, there was a boot print. A clear impression, just the size of a boy Jackson's age. Come on. Maybe we can catch up with him."

She started forward, but he grabbed her arm and pulled her back. "You're going to get hurt if you keep floundering around in the dark."

She tipped her head enough to shine her light right in his eyes, fully prepared to tell him he had no right to lecture her as if she were a child. But then she realized all of the redness on his face wasn't due to the cold. She lifted her hand to his cheek, but stopped just short of touching him. "You're bleeding."

He put a hand up and smeared the trickle of blood. "It's nothing. I tripped and fell a little way back."

"You can't just stand there bleeding. Do you have a first aid kit?"

"It's nothing," he repeated. "I'll deal with it back at the cars."

She turned away. "I'm not going back. Not when I finally found Jackson's trail. If he's out here, I'm not going to leave him."

He took out his phone. "I'll make note of the GPS coordinates and we can come out here in the morning, with the search-and-rescue team."

"No. By then it might be too late."

"Lily!"

"Scott!" she mimicked his tone and glared at him. "I'll be fine. I know how to take care of myself, and I have a satellite phone if I run into trouble."

"Where did you get a satellite phone?"

"I borrowed it from a friend."

He drew himself up taller. "I'm ordering you to go back with me."

"Or what? You're only my boss during work hours. And if that's how you're going to act, I don't want to work for you anyway."

His shoulders sagged. "Please come with me? I'm not asking as your boss. I'm asking as your friend."

Were they friends? Sometimes it didn't feel that way, and yet who else would be out here with her in the freezing darkness? "I can't," she said. "I can't leave Jackson out here in the cold. What if he's lost, or hurt? What if someone is still after him?"

She couldn't see Scott's expression clearly in the darkness, but he shifted from foot to foot, as if physically wrestling with the problem. Then he hooked his thumbs beneath the front straps of his pack. "Then let's get going and see where this trail leads."

Slogging along in full dark now, the thin beams from their headlamps scarcely penetrating the gloom, they did their best to stay on either side of the trail. The only sounds were the crunch of boots on snow and their own labored breathing. Were they getting any closer to Jackson—or only headed farther away from safety?

A sharp whistle pierced the air, and a rush of wind

brushed past Lily's cheek. Bark flew from the trunk of a tree. Then she was on the ground, flat on her stomach in the snow with Scott on top of her. He was big and heavy, crushing the breath out of her. She raised her head to yell at him to get off of her, but he shoved her back into the snow. He spoke softly, his mouth next to her ear. "Stay down! That was a gunshot."

Chapter Thirteen

Lily froze, heart pounding painfully. Someone was shooting at them?

"Turn off your headlamp," Scott whispered, and his own light went out.

"I can't move," she said.

Scott slid off of her to lie beside her. He was breathing hard, and he kept one hand firmly on her back, as if prepared to shove her down once more. "Turn it off now," he whispered.

She did so. "Why is someone shooting at us?" she asked, keeping her voice low.

"I don't know. But they came too close to hitting us for me to think it was a random shot. They could have a night vision scope or goggles or something."

She started to ask him how he knew that, then remembered he had been in the military. "What are we going to do?" she asked. "We can't just lie here and wait for him to find us."

"We're going to have to crawl." He turned his head to one side, then pointed in that direction. "Over that way. The tree cover is more dense."

The trees were growing so close together they had to squeeze through them, negotiating an obstacle course of tree roots, trunks, rocks and thick snow. By the time they reached the massive trunk of a fallen lodgepole pine, she was sodden with melted snow and shivering from the cold. "When I give the word, vault over this log and flatten yourself behind it," Scott said.

"Okay." She tensed, waiting. After what seemed like an eternity, but was probably only a few seconds, he said, "Now!"

She pulled herself up onto the log, while he pushed from behind. On the other side, she flattened herself to the ground, pushing up under the tree for a few inches. Scott landed just past her and did the same.

She strained her ears to hear the sound of anyone approaching, but her head was too full of her own ragged breathing and the pounding of her heartbeat. "I don't hear anyone," Scott said after a long moment.

"I don't either." Then a terrifying thought made her raise her head. "Where are the dogs?"

Scott shoved her down once more. "Stay down!"

"Where are the dogs?" she asked again. "If whoever that was shot Shelby or Hunter…"

"They both ran off when the gunshot was fired," he said. "It probably terrified them."

The shot had terrified her. But now she was just angry. "If he hurt my dog…"

"I know," Scott said. "Don't think about that now."

She lay with her face to the ground, shivering hard now, colder than she had ever been in her life. "He won't have to shoot us," she muttered. "We'll freeze to death, lying here."

"Shhh. Someone's coming."

Panic squeezed at her, and she had to bite her lip hard enough to taste blood in order to keep from crying out. Something was definitely shuffling toward them, but it didn't sound like a person exactly. More like an animal. Or a couple of animals.

Shelby, then Hunter, climbed over the fallen tree and began licking their faces, tails wagging. Lily pulled Shelby down beside her and held the squirming dog tightly, imagining at any moment that another bullet would come their way.

But all was silent.

Hunter lay beside Scott, panting softly. After a long while, Scott raised one ski pole into the air. Then the other. Nothing happened. He raised a hand. Nothing.

Finally, he sat up. "I think whoever was out there left."

"Why did they leave?" She wanted to stay down, safe, but feared freezing to death almost as much as she feared the person with the gun. Stiffly, she pushed into a sitting position. Shelby jumped up and shook.

"Maybe they realized we weren't who they were after," Scott said.

It took a moment before her fear-and-frost-numbed brain realized what he meant. "Do you think he's looking for Jackson?"

"Maybe you aren't the only one who didn't believe he died in that avalanche."

"Oh." The single syllable came out like a moan. "Jackson's dad said he thinks people from another country might be behind all this."

"If that's true, they could be really dangerous," Scott said. "But why does he think that?"

"They've contacted him before. Two people beat him up the night I was babysitting. That's how he got the black eye. They told him if he didn't hand over the information they wanted they would kill him. But when he didn't back down, they kidnapped Jackson."

"What do they want?"

"I can't tell you—I promised. He said it was top secret."

"Why didn't he tell the sheriff this?" Scott asked.

"He doesn't trust the sheriff's department. But he doesn't want to involve the FBI, either."

"Why not?"

She rubbed her hands together, trying to get circulation into her numb fingers. "He wouldn't say, but I wonder if it isn't because he's thinking he'll have to cooperate with the kidnappers to get his son back. He doesn't want to, but he would do anything to save Jackson. What parent wouldn't?"

"Does Endicott know who is behind this?" Scott asked. "Specific people, I mean."

"No. But this morning when I picked up the satellite phone he told me he's afraid it might be someone in his household. Or someone who works for him. Otherwise, how did they know Jackson would be skiing the day he was taken?"

"They could have had someone watching the house," Scott said. "It's easy enough to see people loading up and driving away with skis on top of the vehicle."

"That's true. He's being careful, all the same."

"I don't blame him for that." He stood, then held out his hand. "Come on. We need to get moving and warm up. We should think about where we're going to spend the night."

She took his hand and let him pull her to her feet. Exhaustion had rolled in as the fear receded. She was shivering with cold and clumsy with stiffness.

"Here." Scott shoved something into her hands. "Eat this."

"I'm okay," she said, and tried to push him away.

"When was the last time you ate?" he asked.

"I had a protein bar a few hours ago," she said.

"Your blood sugar is probably dropping. Eat."

She looked at the item in your hand. "A candy bar? Really?"

"It has nuts in it and chocolate. Quick sugar. Eat it."

"Sheesh. You are so bossy!" But she peeled off the wrapper and took a bite, and had to suppress a groan. When had anything tasted so good?

While she ate, he gave the dogs treats and consulted his phone. "Looks like we're headed toward Pandora," he said.

"The tracks seemed to be leading that way."

He looked around them, at the impenetrable darkness. "Jackson has a forty-eight-hour head start on us. He could be at Pandora by now."

She finished the last of the candy bar, crumpled the wrapper and tucked it into the pocket of her parka. "If he thought of heading to Pandora, don't you think whoever is after him thought of that, too?"

"Maybe. But we can't do anything about that tonight. Right now, we need to find a place to spend the night."

"What about right here?" She looked at the flattened space where they had been lying. "I don't want to lose Jackson's trail."

He looked around. "I'd feel better if we moved into denser brush," he said. "We need a fire to try to warm up, but we need to keep it hidden."

"Fine. Just remember where the trail is so we can pick it up in the morning."

She followed him into a section of woods choked with scrub oak and service berry, the dense network of twigs and branches grabbing at her clothing like bony fingers. They came to a bowl-shaped depression maybe six feet in diameter. "This should do," he said. He dropped his pack, pulled out a knife, and began hacking at the scrub around them. "I'll build a shelter. See if you can gather some wood for a fire."

She was so exhausted all she wanted to do was drop where she stood, but she made herself turn away in search of wood. Everything she found was wet with snow, but by digging into the undergrowth she was able to snag a few drier pieces. By the time she returned, Scott had constructed a lean-to and spread a tarp on the ground in its shelter. He was arranging rocks in a circle for a fire ring. She dropped the wood she had collected beside him, removed her pack, and took out her sleeping bag and a pair of dry socks.

With dry feet, and seated on the insulating sleeping bag, she began to feel better. Scott got a fire going, using a lighter and fire starters from his pack, then he set snow to melt in a small coffeepot. She dug into her pack and pulled out the food she had brought with her and contributed to the pile of provisions he had unearthed from his own supplies. The dogs moved in close, sniffing at everything with interest.

"You were prepared to spend the night out," he said.

"I didn't want to, but I knew I would if I thought I was close to finding Jackson."

He nodded and fed each dog a piece of jerky. Shelby brought hers over to the sleeping bag and lay beside Lily. "I take it Mr. Endicott thinks more than one person is involved in the kidnapping—not just the man who was killed?" Scott asked.

"It looks that way." She took off one glove and buried her hand in the dog's thick ruff of fur. "Especially if whoever was shooting at us was after Jackson."

"We don't know that."

"No, but how many other criminals are out here in the wilderness?"

He fed larger branches into the fire. "What could be so

important a whole group of people would take such a big risk? They're bound to know everyone will be searching for a missing kid."

"You and I are the only ones searching for Jackson right now."

"I thought Endicott was a software developer. What could kidnappers want from that?"

"You're not going to let this go, are you?"

"I'm just trying to make sense of things."

"Endicott Industries has a lot of government contracts," she said.

He looked at her. The light from the fire lit one side of his face with an orange glow, highlighting the hard line of his jaw and the strong jut of his nose. The other half of his face was all darkness, his expression unreadable. "Are they military contracts?" he asked.

"I can't say."

He nodded. "I get the picture. What else did Endicott tell you?"

"He said Jackson had gone fishing and hiking and stuff like that, but nothing more." She stared out into the darkness. There were so many ways to get hurt out here—the cold, a fall, attacks by animals—both four- and two-legged.

"He's a nine-year-old kid," Scott said.

"A really smart kid."

"But a kid."

"Why are you like this?"

He sat up straighter. "Like what?"

"Always assuming the worst. Why can't you wait to pronounce him done for until we know for sure?"

"You can't go around blind to reality. Most of the time things don't turn out for the best."

"But sometimes they do. I'm not naive, but I'm not going to give up too soon."

He said nothing, but turned to the stack of provisions. "I'm going to make us something hot to drink. We'll both feel a lot better when we've had some food."

He made hot chocolate and filled two mugs, then they ate ham and cheese sandwiches. The cocoa and the food did make her feel better. "Thanks for pushing me down earlier," she said. "You probably saved my life."

"Sorry if I was too rough."

"You didn't hurt me. I guess you recognized gunfire right away because of your experiences in the war."

"Yeah."

"Do you ever have, like, flashbacks?" Was that too personal a question to ask?

"Not in a long time."

Had war made him cynical? Or was that just his nature? He wasn't the first person to accuse her of being too optimistic—that was her nature.

He repacked the rest of their provisions and rinsed the mugs with hot water from the kettle. She stared into the fire, sleep dragging at her. She was trying to work up the energy to say good night and crawl into her sleeping bag when he said, "I'm sorry I was so hard on you yesterday."

The apology startled her awake. "I'm not some fragile flower who's going to wilt when someone yells at me," she said.

"Did I yell?"

"No. You were just a little…brusque."

"Sorry." He smoothed his hand down Hunter's side. Both dogs were already asleep, curled by the fire and snoring. "I've always been better with dogs than people."

"Maybe when I've been doing this work as long as you

have, I'll be more cynical, too," she said. "But I'm not there yet."

"This work didn't make me cynical. Not really."

"What did?"

He didn't answer. Maybe that was the question that was too personal to answer.

"Maybe it's just my disposition," he said. "Or the war—I lost people I cared about over there. And then I lost Clark."

"Your friend who died in the avalanche."

"Yeah. Add that I've never pulled a live person from a snowslide, and I guess that has made me cynical."

"I get it. You don't have to apologize. And neither do I." She shrugged. "We feel what we feel."

"I hope you're the one who's right in this case. About Jackson, I mean."

"Yeah, me too." She crawled into her sleeping bag and lay down, waiting for warmth and sleep. She thought of Jackson, and sent up a silent prayer that he was somewhere warm and safe. And that tomorrow they would find him, and everything would be all right.

Chapter Fourteen

Scott woke next to Lily, his arms wrapped tightly around her. The floral scent of her hair teased him to consciousness, then he became aware of the hard line of her spine, pressed against him, and the soft curve of her bottom. She was curled into a fetal position, buried deep in her sleeping bag, a ball of warmth in the frigid predawn. Shelby lay on Lily's other side, so that she was sandwiched between his warmth and the dog's.

Not that he was very warm. Hunter had moved to lie beside what was left of the campfire. Scott couldn't feel his toes or his fingers, and every few minutes a violent shiver rocked him.

He carefully extricated himself from around her. She stirred. "You okay?" he asked.

The sleeping bag wriggled and shifted, then her head emerged. Her face was puffy, hair a wild tangle hiding half her features. She looked soft and vulnerable and younger than her years. "I'm cold."

"Yeah. I'll get the fire started."

When he had a blaze going, she fought the rest of the way out of her sleeping bag and staggered to her feet. "Be right back," she mumbled, and shuffled off into the woods.

By the time she returned, he had the kettle over the

flames and both dogs were eating the kibble he had packed. "I'm going to give them the first water I melt," he said. "Then I'll heat some for us."

"I've got instant coffee crystals," she said. "And oatmeal and peanut butter."

"I've got boiled eggs."

She made a face. "Don't those get crushed in your pack?"

He shrugged. "They're good protein. And I don't care what they look like. I'm going to eat them anyway."

The coffee, when it was finally ready, was scalding hot. The warmth spread through him, driving the last of the sleep from his brain and making him feel halfway human. They ate, the cold making them ravenous. Even oatmeal—not his favorite—tasted good when he was this hungry.

Breakfast over, he stood. "If you'll pack up everything, I'm going to look around a little bit," he said.

"What are you looking for?"

"I want to see if I can find some sign of whoever was shooting at us."

He moved away from the clearing where they had sheltered, both dogs accompanying him. He crossed over the trail they had been following yesterday. The brush thinned, giving way to thick stands of aspens, slender white trunks all leaning slightly to one side, like grass bent by the wind. He studied the snow, which was thinner here, until he found what he was looking for—a single boot print. Not a ski boot, but with lug soles, like a hiking or work boot. Another partial print farther on. He moved more slowly now, carefully placing each step, trying to be as silent as possible. The rising sun slanting through the trees glinted on something at the base of one aspen trunk. Scott bent to look and found two brass shell casings. Forty-five caliber. A new cold slithered up his spine. Too close for comfort. Had the shooter spent the night nearby? He could have killed them in their sleep.

He took out his phone, intending to note the GPS coordinates of this location, but the device had switched itself off and refused to power up again. He swore to himself. Why hadn't he remembered that cold drained batteries? He should have slept with the phone next to him in his sleeping bag instead of stuffed into the side of his pack. He hoped Lily had been smarter.

He went a little farther, but saw no more boot prints or shell casings. No sign of a camp. The shooter must have moved on after he had determined they weren't a threat. Maybe he had decided they were a couple of hikers or skiers out for adventure. Maybe he decided to leave before they spotted him.

He returned to camp. Lily had packed up their belongings and was scooping snow over the fire to douse it. "Did you find anything?" she asked.

He shook his head. He'd keep the information about the bullets to himself for now. "Let's keep heading toward Pandora," he said. "Maybe we'll find Jackson there."

"It's a week today since he was taken," she said. "That's a long time to be out in this cold."

"The kidnapper was probably taking care of him before he was killed," Scott said. "We found their camp, with a fire and shelter."

"But now Jackson is out here without a pack or anyone to help."

"Don't think about that," he said. "Just focus on finding him."

They picked up where they had left off, following the trail of disturbed snow. It could have been a trail made by a boy, but it could have just as easily been a path followed by wildlife—mule deer or elk or even moose. They saw no more boot prints, nothing to tell them for sure that they were on the right track.

The trail ended abruptly, at the base of a large pine, the furrowed reddish bark bright against the paler aspen and white snow. Shelby barked, then planted her front feet against the trunk of the tree. The dog stared up into the limbs, then barked again.

"What is it, girl?" Lily asked.

Scott craned his head to look up into the tree. The branches were thick, a tangle of needles so dark they were almost black. "I don't see anything," he said. "Maybe she treed a squirrel. Come on, Hunter." He turned to move on.

"Wait!" Lily said. She shifted position, craning her neck. "Jackson, is that you? It's me, Lily."

The tree limbs shifted and a pale face—familiar to Scott from the posters stuck up everywhere around the resort—poked out. "Lily! What are you doing here?"

"We're looking for you," she said. "We've come to take you home."

The boy started crying. He was sobbing so hard Scott was afraid he was going to fall out of the tree. "Do you need help getting down from there?" Scott asked.

The boy sniffed and frowned at Scott. "Who are you?"

"This is Scott Linden," Lily said. "He's head of ski patrol. Remember? I introduced you one time."

Shelby barked again. Hunter came to stand beside them and he started barking also. "You'd better come down," Lily said. "The dogs aren't going to quiet down until you do."

"Let me help." Scott reached up toward the boy.

"I can do it." Jackson slowly began climbing down. When he reached the ground, he turned to face them. Strands of blond hair stuck out from beneath his ski helmet. His cheeks were red and streaked with dirt. His blue parka was dirty, too, with a jagged rip in the front. Lily pulled him into a hug. "I'm so glad to see you," she said. "We were so worried."

He squirmed, and she loosened her hold on him and stepped back. "Oh my gosh—you're bleeding!" She pointed to his hand.

The boy looked down at the bare hand, at the gash on the web of flesh between his thumb and forefinger. He flexed his fingers. "It's not that bad," he said.

"What happened to you?" she asked. "Why do you only have one glove?"

"I dropped the other one somewhere."

"We found your pack," she said. "Why did you leave it behind?"

He shifted from foot to foot, eyes darting, not fixing on any one point. "I can tell you all of that later. Can we get out of here now?"

"We'll go," Scott said. "But you need a couple of things first." He removed his pack and dug out a spare pair of gloves and another candy bar. He passed these items, and a bottle of water, over to Jackson.

"Thanks." Jackson tore into the candy bar and ate it in four bites, then chugged the water. He handed the empty bottle to Scott. "When I realized I'd dropped a glove, I wanted to go back and look for it, but I was too afraid. I was terrified they'd find it and be able to track me."

"Who would find it?" Lily asked.

"The people who've been after me. One of them even took a couple of shots at me last night. That was before I went up the tree. I guess they lost my trail in the dark and didn't see me up there."

"Come on." Scott put his hand on the boy's shoulder. The kid's story was making him nervous. "Let's get moving." He wanted to put some distance between Jackson's hiding place and themselves, in case the kidnappers were tracking him again in daylight. Which they would surely do. It sounded like they'd been pretty stubborn about keeping after the kid.

He led the way, Jackson behind him and Lily bringing up the rear, the dogs ranged between them. They were leaving a pretty big track through the woods that would be easy to follow. He glanced over his shoulder at Jackson. "How many people are after you?" he asked.

"Just the one guy, now that DJ is dead. But I'm pretty sure there are others. DJ was taking me somewhere, I just don't know where."

"Who is DJ?" Scott asked.

"The guy who grabbed me at the ski resort. That's what he told me to call him. I don't know what DJ stands for."

"He died in the avalanche?" Lily asked.

"Yeah. He triggered the avalanche when we were crossing this big snowfield. I guess I was lucky—I was on the very edge of the slide and it kind of tossed me off into the woods."

"You left your backpack behind," Lily said.

"I didn't want to, but I figured I had to. I knew DJ had friends. He had been in touch with them a couple of times on a satellite telephone. I thought if they came looking and found my backpack, they would think I had died in the avalanche, too."

"What was DJ doing with you out here in the wilderness all this time?" Lily asked. Scott had been wondering this, too. Even given the weather and the terrain, Jackson and his captor should have been able to reach Pandora in two or three days at most. Or they could have hiked to a road, where an accomplice could pick them up.

"We walked and camped." Jackson scowled. "At first, he tried to make it sound like we were on a big, fun adventure.

But it was just cold and boring. The last couple of days he was begging whoever was on the other end of the phone to come and get us. But they told him we had to stay out here until they told us we could come in. DJ said they were waiting for my dad to pay the ransom." His face crumpled. "I couldn't understand why he didn't just pay."

"Oh, honey." Lily held him close. "Your dad has spent every spare minute trying to find you."

Jackson pulled away from her and scrubbed at his eyes with his fists. He sniffed, then said, "After the avalanche, I was worried Dad would think I had died, too. I decided I needed to hike out to a road or a house or someplace where I could get help. But I ended up getting disoriented in the woods and wandering around for a long time. And then somebody started shooting and I climbed that tree."

"That was smart," Lily said.

"It was freezing cold, and I was scared if I didn't die by gunshot, I'd die falling out of the tree and breaking my neck."

"You're safe now," Lily said.

"Do you have a gun?" Jackson asked.

"I don't," Lily said.

"What about him?"

Scott assumed this referred to him. He looked back over his shoulder. "I have a gun," he said. "I hope I don't have to use it."

"The guys who are after me have guns," Jackson said. "DJ forced me to come with him by threatening to shoot me."

Scott looked past Jackson to Lily. His gaze met hers, and she raised both eyebrows, eyes wide.

He faced forward again. "We'll just have to avoid the

people with guns," he said. And night vision scopes and who knew what else.

"I could call for help on my satellite phone," Lily said. "I should call your dad and let him know you're okay."

"That's a good idea," Scott said. "Where are you going to tell the cavalry to meet us?"

She glanced around them. "We can give them our GPS coordinates, right?"

"My phone battery died sometime last night," he said. "What about yours?"

She fumbled with her pack and pulled out her phone. "I turned it off last night to save battery." She pressed the button on the side, but nothing happened. "I can't get it back on."

"Below-freezing temperatures drain batteries," he said.

"Maybe they can triangulate our location from the sat phone signal," she said. "Or we could tell them we're headed to Pandora and they can meet us there."

"That's not a bad idea," Scott said. "We can probably make it to Pandora in three or four hours." He didn't think they were far from the last ridge before the ghost town, but it would take a while to make that climb. "Are you up to walking that far?" he asked Jackson. The boy looked dead on his feet.

Jackson lifted his chin and squared his shoulders. "I'll walk as far as I have to to get away from those guys."

Lily took out the satellite phone and switched it on. "At least this battery hasn't died," she said after a moment when the phone lit up. She waited, frowning at the screen. "It's searching for a signal."

"You may have to wait until we get out of these trees to make a call," Scott said. "Satellite phones need a clear line of sight to the sky."

She continued to study the phone. "It says it's unable to connect."

"Switch it off, and you can try again when we're on the ridge, without as much tree cover," Scott said.

They trudged on, heads down, not talking. Lily tried warming her cell phone next to her body, but if still refused to turn on. They made slow progress, all three of them too exhausted to hurry. She kept an eye on Jackson, who walked just in front of her. The boy stumbled from time to time, practically asleep on his feet, but he refused any suggestion that he needed help.

Scott had an old-fashioned compass to navigate, and kept them headed toward Pandora. They began to climb the ridge that separated the old mining town from this more wooded terrain, and the tree cover began to thin. Lily tried not to think what a target they might present for anyone watching them through binoculars—or a spotting scope.

"Let's stop a minute and have some more food and water," Scott said after a while. He halted in the shelter of a car-sized boulder, and they crouched behind it, hidden from view. Within a minute, Jackson was shivering again, and Lily removed the extra clothing she had brought with her from her pack and handed it to him. "I'm sorry I didn't remember before now," she said.

He removed his jacket to pull on the sweatshirt, and as he did so, the sleeve of the fleece top he wore beneath his jacket slid up, revealing a purpling bruise. "What happened there?" she asked.

He shoved the sleeve down over the bruise. "I refused to go with DJ, so he dragged me along." He rubbed at his side. "He jammed the gun pretty hard in my ribs. There's probably a bruise there, too."

"How did you cut your finger?" Lily asked.

"I was trying to start a fire by rubbing sticks together. I've read about it, but it's a lot harder than it looks. I jammed a sharp stick into my hand and never did get a fire going."

Lily took his hand and examined the injury. "You can't let that get infected. Let me get the first aid kit." She pulled out the first aid supplies and began tending the hand.

To distract the boy, Scott crouched in front of him. "Do you know who was working with DJ?" he asked.

"I don't know. DJ complained about getting stuck out in the middle of nowhere with me while everyone else got to sit around in a cushy rental."

"Why take you out into the wilderness anyway?" Lily asked as she dabbed antibiotic ointment onto the wound.

"DJ said nobody would ever look for me out here. They'd look for the kidnapper to get away in a car, not on skis. And even if they did figure out we were here, we'd be hard to find, with all the trees and snow. I guess he thought it was a pretty smart idea, until we were actually out here freezing and falling over logs and stuff."

"We saw your tracks that first afternoon," Scott said. "And we had a helicopter up looking right after that."

"I heard the helicopter," he said. "I wanted to find a way to signal to it, but DJ was watching me too closely."

Lily stuck a bandage on his hand, then closed the lid of the first aid kit. "That should keep it from getting infected."

"Thanks." Jackson pulled on the gloves Scott had given him. There were much too big, but warm. "Where are we going now?"

"Pandora is closest," Scott said.

"That old ghost town?" Jackson asked. "Is it near here?"

"Just on the other side of a ridge," Scott said. "There are buildings there we can shelter in."

"Won't the kidnappers know that, too?" Jackson asked. "We could get there and find them waiting."

"We could, but other people go there, too," Scott said. "Even in winter, it's a popular destination for cross-country skiers. And I'm pretty sure there are no fancy rentals there. Once we get there, we can call for help. We'll have shelter where we can wait."

"I hope we can get someone to meet us there," Lily said. She took out the satellite phone again and switched it on. After a few seconds, a grin erased the weariness on her face. "We have a connection." She punched in a number. "I'm calling your dad," she told Jackson.

"Hello?" The man on the other end of the phone spoke so loudly and clearly Scott and Jackson could both hear him.

"Denny?" Lily asked.

"This is Mike. Lily, is that you? Are you okay?"

"Mike? Why are you answering Denny's personal phone? Is he okay?"

"He's tied up with something else right now, but he asked me to monitor his personal phone in case you or Jackson called. We've been worried sick."

"Jackson is with me now. That's why I'm calling."

"Is Jackson all right? Where are you?"

"He's fine. We're both fine."

"Thank God for that. Where are you?"

"We're near Nickel Ridge," she said. "We're on our way to Pandora."

"Pandora. That's great. I'll send someone right away."

"Let the sheriff know what's going on. And the resort? I'm sure people are wondering where I am. And Scott Linden. He's with us."

"Don't worry about a thing. I'll take care of it. You get to Pandora and you'll be safe. I'm so glad you called. Denny is going to be overjoyed. Now let me make some calls and get you taken care of."

Lily took the phone from her ear. "He hung up before I could talk to Denny or ask him any questions," she said.

"It doesn't matter," Scott said. "He'll send help. All we have to do is get to Pandora. We don't have much farther to go."

Lily looked up, at the low bank of clouds moving in. "It looks like we could get more snow," she said.

"Then let's get moving." Scott stood and slipped on his pack. "Let's try to get ahead of the storm."

Lily stowed the phone and donned her own pack, then the three of them, plus the two dogs, set out again. The route grew steeper, devoid of trees or even brush. "We don't have far to go now," Scott said. "We should be able see Pandora from the top."

It began to snow, big, soft flakes flitting down. But the scattering of flakes became a deluge, and wind blew the snow sideways. It hit their faces like shards of ice, and the swirling snow blinded them. The flakes piled in miniature drifts on their shoulders and the tops of their helmets, and soon obscured the rocky ground. At every breath, Lily inhaled snow. "Do you even know where we're going?" she gasped.

"Just keep climbing," Scott said. "We should be more sheltered on the other side of this ridge."

At last, they reached the top of the ridge. They paused and looked down the other side. "Do you see Pandora?" Jackson asked.

Lily couldn't see anything but snow. All that white could be covering boulders or buildings—at this point, she couldn't tell.

"I think it's over this direction," Scott said, and raised his arm to point.

A thud, like a fist punching a pillow, made a dull, hollow sound. Scott grunted, then sank to his knees. A second dull thud sounded to his right, and Lily recognized the sound of a bullet striking a target. She screamed and shoved Jackson to the ground. "Scott!" she shouted. "Scott, what happened?"

"Stay down," he said, his voice surprisingly calm.

She stayed down, but she crawled toward him. "What happened?" she asked.

"Stay away," he cautioned. "I've been shot."

Chapter Fifteen

Scott lay prone in the snow, fighting to breathe, heart drumming painfully in his chest. He braced himself against the pain he expected—but felt nothing. With one hand he probed at his chest, but found no exit wound. No blood. His back hurt as if he had been punched. Careful to stay low, he felt at his back. His fingers found a hole in his backpack, the coffeepot beneath it, dented now. There was still no pain, and he could move freely, now that he had caught his breath.

"Are you all right?" Lily asked from her spot, prone in the snow a few feet to his left. Jackson lay beside her—the dogs were nowhere in sight.

"I think so." He rose up on all fours. "I think the bullet struck the coffeepot in my pack. I don't think I'm bleeding."

"There's a hole in your backpack," she said.

"Yeah." He started to his feet, intending to remove the backpack and examine it more closely, but another shot rang out, sending him flat to the ground once more. A quick glance around told him they were in a terrible position—pinned down on the side of the ridge, easily standing out from the snow. But just downslope was a grove of small trees, and below that even deeper woods. All they needed was a chance to get to cover.

"On the count of three, I want you both to jump up and

run as fast as you can for that grove of trees just below us and to the left," he said. "Can you do that?"

"What are you going to do?" she asked.

"I'm going to fire in the direction I think those shots came from. The shooter will focus on me instead of the two of you and you can get away."

"Scott!" she protested. "They'll shoot you."

"No they won't." They might, but he wasn't going to think about that. "I'll stay down. You and Jackson have to get away. Promise me you'll run."

"All right." She didn't sound enthusiastic, but he was counting on her putting the boy's safety first.

"Jackson?" he asked.

"Yes," the boy said, his voice a little shaky, but clear. "I'll run."

Scott found the gun, checked that it was loaded and clicked off the safety. "On the count of three," he said. "One, two, three." He fired twice up the slope. A shot immediately answered, striking the ground to his left. He army-crawled a few feet upslope and fired again. More return fire, though again only a single shot. Was the shooter conserving ammunition?

Scott looked over his shoulder to where Lily and Jackson had been huddled together. They were no longer there. He waited, counting to a hundred. Time to get himself out of here.

He slid the pistol into the waistband of his pants, snugged against the small of his back. Then he grabbed the pack firmly by the sides. "One. Two. Three." He hoisted the pack over his head. Another bullet tore the pack from his hand. He flung the pack to one side, shoved to his feet and ran. He fully expected to feel a bullet slam into him at any moment, but no impact came. He stumbled through the thick snow in his boots, scrambling for purchase, trying to stay low, aiming for the grove of trees.

He crashed into the copse of trees, snow flying from the branches of pinion trees. "Over here!" Lily cried.

She was crouched at the base of an ancient juniper, the trunk two feet in diameter, feathery branches weighted down by snow forming an umbrella over her. He moved in beside her. "I had to leave my pack," he said, gasping for breath.

"Better your pack than the rest of you."

"Where's Jackson?" he asked.

"I don't know," she said. "He was ahead of me, and then I couldn't see him anymore." She raised her head. "Jackson! Jackson, where are you?"

No answer. "Hunter!" Scott shouted.

"Shelby!" Lily called. She whistled and clapped, but the snow absorbed all sound before it went very far.

"We can't go on without Jackson and the dogs." Her voice was tight with fear.

He gripped her arm. "Jackson probably just ran ahead of us. Maybe the dogs are with him." He was trying to comfort her, and himself, too. After all the trouble they had gone to to find him, surely they couldn't have lost the boy now.

Snow continued to fall, hard. Lily turned a complete circle, peering into the wall of white. "How are we ever going to find them?" she asked, sounding as if she might burst into tears.

Scott nudged her. "We need to get out of here before someone comes looking for us. It won't be difficult for them to find us." Even with the heavy snow, they were close enough to the top of the ridge that it probably wouldn't be that far for whoever had fired those shots to come after them.

"What if they have Jackson?" she asked.

"Then we can't help him if we let them find us, too."

He reloaded the gun, then led the way down the slope, moving in a zigzag path from the cover of tree to tree. Periodically they stopped, and he strained his ears, listening for sounds of pursuit. But the woods around them were silent except for the occasional soft "whump" as a tree released its burden of snow. At least the continued snowfall did a good job of erasing their tracks.

They headed steadily downhill, stumbling and stopping to help each other up. Scott searched for any sign that Jackson and the dogs had come this way, but found nothing.

"Stop!" Lily called when they had been trudging along for a quarter of an hour. She pulled her pack to the front and began rummaging in it. "I'm going to call the sheriff and let them know what happened, see if I can find out where our rescuers are."

"Good idea." Scott looked around them, seeing nothing in the swirling snow. He felt half naked without his pack. Maybe he'd made a mistake, sacrificing it that way. He hadn't had any food left in it, but he had first aid supplies and his sleeping bag.

"I can't find the phone."

Lily's words jerked him out of his stupor. "What do you mean you can't find it?"

"It's not in my pack. I swear I stowed it back in here after I spoke with Mike."

"Where did you put the phone?" Scott asked.

"In the outside pocket." She indicated the pocket.

"Was it unfastened like that?" Scott asked.

"I thought I closed it, but it was open when I went to look for the phone." She met his gaze. "I fell a couple of times. Maybe it came out then."

He looked back the way they had come, at an expanse

of smooth white, their tracks already buried under fresh snowfall. Finding a phone that had fallen in all that could take hours, or even days. And they still might never find it.

"What are we going to do?" Lily looked at Scott, her expression bereft.

"I don't think we can risk going back to Pandora," he said. "I think the kidnappers were probably the ones shooting at us. They probably figured Pandora was the closest place for us to seek shelter and stationed a guard on the ridge to watch for us."

"But the sheriff and his officers should be in Pandora soon," Lily said. "They should be able to deal with the kidnappers."

"Maybe the snow has delayed them," Scott said. "They could be waiting on a SWAT team or other reinforcements."

"I'm not sure I want to find them if we have to tell them we lost Jackson," she said. "What if the kidnappers found him first? What if they hurt Jackson? What if they hurt the dogs?"

He put his arm around her. "The only way we're going to get out of this is to stay calm," he said.

She leaned into him, head on his shoulder. She was trembling slightly—was that from cold or fear, or something else? After a moment, she looked up at him. "When you were in the army did you ever feel scared and hopeless?"

"I was afraid plenty of times," he said. "Anyone who says they aren't is lying. But I never let myself feel hopeless. I had too many other people depending on me for that."

She pressed her lips tightly together, then nodded. "Right. Jackson is depending on us. Denny and Mike and all the people who care about Jackson, too. And Hunter and Shelby are depending on us."

She gripped the straps of her pack and looked around

them. The snow had let up a little, but was still falling steadily, the blanket of white obscuring most features of the landscape. "Can you even tell which way we're headed?" she asked.

"If we keep heading downhill, we'll reach the bottom of the ridge," he said.

"Then what?" she asked.

"Then we'll decide what to do next."

She said nothing, but set off again. He hurried to catch up with her. "I don't think anyone is following us," she said.

"It doesn't sound like it, no."

Scott's back hurt, they were almost out of food, and it was only going to get colder as the day wore on. "We'll have to head back toward the ski resort," he said. "The kidnappers are probably counting on us coming back to Pandora, since it's closer. But if we can reach SkyCrest, we should be safe."

"We don't have to go all the way to SkyCrest," she said. "We only have to get to the avalanche site at Axis Ridge. My car is parked near there."

"And Brian's truck is beside your car." At her puzzled look, he added, "I borrowed it from him."

"How long is that going to take?" she asked.

He tried to calculate. They had been out here almost two days already, but part of that time they were unsure of their destination. The terrain and the weather had been against them. He still had his compass, and they would be traveling over territory they had covered before. They would have to stop when darkness set in, but they could set out again at first light tomorrow. "We should be able to make it tomorrow," he said. "We'll push on in as straight a line as possible."

Lily stared at him. He couldn't read her expression, between the goggles shielding her eyes and the fleece gaiter pulled up to her nose. But her shoulders slumped with fatigue, and she was surely as cold as he was. "The sooner we reach the resort, the sooner we can get other people out here looking for Jackson and the dogs," he said.

She nodded. "Right."

They reached the bottom of the ridge—and the almost impenetrable walls of trees. He had hoped to find the path through the woods they had followed before, but fresh snow had obscured their tracks, leaving them to fight their way through the heavy growth, sinking in snow to their knees at times, and tripping over hidden logs and boulders. When she had fallen for the sixth time in an hour, Lily pushed to her feet once more with a curse.

"We need to stop and build a fire," Scott said.

"I thought you said we need to keep going."

"We can't keep going like this. We're both clumsier than usual because we're so cold. We're getting hypothermic. We need to stop, have a hot drink and try to plot a course out of here."

He expected her to argue, but instead, she merely sat down on a snow-covered log and slumped forward, elbows on knees.

He cleared snow from a hollow in front of the log on which she sat, piling more snow in a wall to shield the blaze from the wind. Then he dug beneath a tangle of fallen logs and pulled out drier kindling. "What do you have in your pack to start a fire?" he asked when he had the beginnings of a campfire laid.

She removed the pack and opened it, then pulled out a plastic bag containing a lighter, waterproof matches and an old prescription bottle. He popped the cap on the bottle and found it filled with cotton balls coated in petroleum jelly.

"After you told me what you used as a fire starter, I decided that was a good idea," she said.

He nodded and shoved a couple of the cotton balls in among the kindling and flicked the lighter.

Five minutes later, he was feeding slightly larger pieces of wood into the bright flames. Lily still hadn't moved. "It's going to be okay," he said gently.

"Jackson is nine!" The fierceness of her words had him sitting back on his heels. "He's just a kid. He's cold and hungry and afraid." Her voice choked. "His mom died. His dad works all the time. I was one person who always tried to be there for him and now even I've let him down."

She began to sob. Scott moved onto the log beside her and pulled her close. "You didn't let anyone down," he said. "You couldn't have done anything about whoever was shooting at us. Jackson did the right thing, running away from the shooter. It's no one's fault we got separated in the snowstorm."

She sniffed. "I'm worried about Shelby and Hunter, too. They're cold and hungry. What if they freeze to death?"

"They're both healthy, thick-coated dogs. They won't freeze to death." At least he hoped not. "Our job now is to keep from freezing to death ourselves and get to help."

She said nothing, so after a moment he pulled his arm from around her. "What have you got to eat in your pack?" he asked.

She took out several packets of electrolyte drink powder, the instant coffee, some jerky, plastic pouches of peanut butter, some tea bags and a single metal mug. He considered the array, selected the peanut butter and the electrolyte packets, and the mug. "I'll melt some snow," he said, and stood.

They passed the mug of hot electrolyte drink back and forth between them, and each had a stick of jerky. By the time they were done, Lily was sitting up straighter and Scott could think more clearly. "Are you ready to keep going?" he asked.

"Yes. But which way?" She gestured to the woods surrounding them. "All I can see are trees."

"We still have the compass." He took the instrument from his pocket. "We just have to keep heading east until we reach Axis Ridge."

They set out again, Lily in front, Scott trailing. He sighted in the compass. "Head for that tall ponderosa with the broken limb hanging down," he said.

When they reached the ponderosa, they checked the compass and set a course toward a large blue spruce. So far, keeping due east had been easy. But then they had to fight their way around a thicket of scrub oak and wild roses, the thorny canes of the roses snagging their clothing.

Scott crashed through the underbrush behind her, attempting to keep them on the right path, but after the fourth time he told her she was veering too far left she turned and glared at him. "If you think you can do better, you walk in the front."

He didn't fare much better breaking trail, and by four in the afternoon he was dazed with exhaustion. Lily stumbled after him, silent. All he could see was more trees, trunks sprouting like hair on the head of a giant as far as the eye could see. Which proved how exhausted he was, if he was thinking in those kind of fanciful metaphors. He stopped, and Lily walked right into him.

He caught her by the shoulders to keep her from falling, then just held on to her. "We need to stop," he said.

"Yeah," she said.

"How did Jackson and his kidnapper ever survive out here for a week?" she asked.

"They were really lucky," he said. "And not that bright to have come up with that as a plan."

"I guess if Denny's suspicions are right and a foreign power is behind the attempt to get the weapons technology, maybe they have no concept of what winter is like here. Or what a mountain wilderness is like." She hugged her arms more tightly around herself.

"You'd think they would do more research," he said.

"Maybe greed makes people take shortcuts," she said. "Or they thought it would only take a day or two before Denny would give in to their demands."

If Jackson had frozen to death, or died in the avalanche, would that have ruined the kidnappers' plans? Or would they have gone forward anyway, lying about Jackson's fate? Maybe that's what the note Denton Endicott had received after the avalanche had been—a lie to make him hand over the information the kidnappers wanted.

Scott tended the fire while she rummaged through her pack. "Looks like coffee and peanut butter for dinner," she said. "Or you can have tea." She held up one of the bags.

"Coffee," he said.

"Then I'll have coffee, too," she said. "It's easier to share if we choose the same thing. Besides, I think I need the caffeine."

He sat beside her on a log while they waited for the water in the cup to boil. "I'm trying really hard not to think about Jackson out there alone in the cold," she said. "But I'm not doing a very good job."

He put his arm around her, and she leaned into him. All the boundaries that had made him careful not to touch her in their everyday life had vanished here in the woods. "How are you feeling?" she asked after a moment. "I mean, where you were shot?"

"A little bruised," he said.

"Let me look," she said. "I mean, what if you have a bullet in you after all?"

"I think I'd know if I had a bullet in me."

"I've read that adrenaline can mask pain."

He swiveled so that his back was to her and shed his jacket. The cold air traveled quickly through his fleece and base layer top, and he shivered involuntarily.

But the shivering ceased when Lily pushed his clothing up to his shoulders and trailed her bare fingers up his back. Heat scorched him along the path of her touch. She stroked lightly at a place near the middle of his spine. "There's a bruise here," she said.

"Yeah." Though what he felt wasn't exactly pain. Every part of him had tensed at her touch, fighting the urge to lean into her.

She traced the line of one of his ribs. "You have a scar here," she said.

He had to think a minute to remember. "Rock climbing accident. I was seventeen. Fell and broke a couple of ribs. Decided it wasn't for me." He had lost the capacity to form complete sentences as her hand drifted lower. If her fingers felt this good, he imagined what it would be like to have her kiss her way down his body…

She pulled the shirts down. "You can put your jacket back on now," she said.

THE WEATHER WAS FREEZING, but warmth flooded Lily. The sight of Scott's bare back sent a liquid heat through her. Smooth skin and firm muscle sculpted over a masculine frame left her breathless. Even as she indulged in the sensation of her fingers gliding over him, she longed to touch even more.

She told herself she was being absurd. Inappropriate even, lusting after her boss. But Scott hadn't been authoritarian or demanding today—only kind and encouraging. His bravery made her less daunted by their circumstances. She was still afraid. Still worried and grieving. But being with him comforted her. And thinking about him—how she wanted to pull off the rest of his clothing, kiss her way down his body and have him kiss her—was a welcome distraction from the fears that threatened to overwhelm her.

They shared their meager meal, passing the cup of coffee back and forth between them, then making a second cup. Even without sugar and creamer the bitter caffeine was a welcome jolt, the hot liquid beating back the cold. They built up the fire until it was a roaring blaze, then huddled before it on the fallen log, soaking up the heat. Neither of them mentioned the risk they were taking—that the blaze might lead pursuers to them. But without the warmth of the fire, they would surely freeze to death. "How are you doing?" Scott asked after a while.

"I'm warmer now," she said. "Not as hungry as I was. What about you?"

"I'm okay. Warmer is most important. And the coffee helped, too."

"I take supplies in my pack every year, hiking and skiing," she said. "It's been drilled in to me by every wilderness guide I ever read and every instructor I ever had. But I never had to use them before this week. This is the second time in a few days that I've had to spend the night out when I didn't intend to."

"I've spent nights out on missions," he said. "I stayed out two nights before they found Clark."

His words were matter-of-fact, but she heard the loss behind them. "Were you alone?"

“I didn’t really want to be around anyone else.”

“After my brother, Ben, died, I didn’t want to talk to anyone else either,” she said. “It’s like grief put a wall between me and other people. I was angry that Ben was gone—and angry at everyone else because they couldn’t understand how much I hurt.”

“I was mostly angry at myself. That I couldn’t save him.”

She wanted to tell him his friend’s death wasn’t his fault. But people always said things like that to suffering people, and the words didn’t help. Instead, she slipped her hand into his and leaned on his arm. He held on tightly. They didn’t say anything for a long time. The fire popped and sent up orange sparks, and the wet wood on the edge of the blaze sizzled and steamed. She breathed in the sweet, smoky aroma of burning pinion and juniper and felt her eyes drifting shut.

“We should try to get some sleep,” Scott said. He unwound his fingers from hers.

“We should share my sleeping bag,” she said. His was with his pack, up on the ridge.

“I’ll just sit up and tend the fire.”

“That’s ridiculous.” She stood and grabbed the bag from her pack, unrolled and unzipped it and spread it by the fire. “Two of us will generate more heat than one.” Then she bit her lip, holding back laughter at her unintentional joke.

Maybe he was thinking the same thing. She thought his cheeks flushed, though perhaps that was merely from the cold. She turned her back to him and stripped down to socks and thermal top and pants, then lay down on the sleeping bag and beckoned him. “Come on. If I let you freeze to death I’ll never get out of these woods.”

Chapter Sixteen

Scott's expression in the firelight was grim, but he peeled down to his long underwear and slid in beside her. With the bag mostly zipped it was a tight fit, but if they spooned together they could manage. It was comfortable even, and much warmer.

Those classes she had taken had taught that this was what people did to survive in the cold. But they never talked about the intimacy of lying with her bottom snugged against his crotch, his very evident erection pressed against her in a way that had her struggling to control her breathing. She wriggled, trying to get comfortable, and heard his gasp. At this rate, neither of them was going to sleep tonight.

She reached back and took his hand and wrapped his arm around her, his fingers splayed across her stomach. "Maybe this isn't such a good idea," he said, his voice soft in her ear.

"Are you saying you won't respect me in the morning?" She meant it as a joke, but part of her was serious. If she gave in to desire and had sex with him tonight, would it jeopardize her job?

"I will always respect you," he said. "But how will you feel about me?"

She wanted to turn and face him, to try to read the expression in his eyes. But that was impossible to do in the confines of the sleeping bag. "Scott, I don't know what's going to happen tomorrow," she said. "All I know is that right now, I want you." To make sure he got the message, she guided his hand down, toward her crotch. He cupped her hard, and she caught her breath before releasing a long sigh.

He kissed her neck, and his tongue traced the line of her collarbone. "Maybe I've been harder on you than everyone else because I was afraid of how much I'm attracted to you," he said. His voice was low and rough, abrading her nerves. She squirmed against him, and he squeezed her hip, stilling her.

"You're…attracted to me?" she asked, the last word a squeak as he gently rolled her nipple between his thumb and forefinger.

"I've had dreams about you." He slid his hand beneath her shirt and cupped her breast.

"What kind of dreams?"

"Inappropriate ones."

All she could do was moan as he slid his hand down her body, coming to rest between her legs once more. When he didn't do anything more, she ground against him. "I need you to touch me," she said.

He pressed his forehead against the back of her head, breathing hard. "I want that. More than anything right now. But are you sure?"

"Yes. Yes, I'm sure." When he didn't answer, she added, "We're two consenting adults. There's nothing in our employment contracts that says we can't be together, and it's certainly not against the law. And if you do ever try to take advantage of me at work—my dad's a lawyer and he'll sue you for everything you have."

He laughed, a deep, sexy chuckle that had her squirming back against him. He slid his hand beneath the waistband of her long underwear bottoms and began to fondle her. She closed her eyes, seeing stars. He was kissing her neck again, doing amazing things with his fingers. Then he slid one finger into her, and she dug the nails of one hand into his thigh. He stilled. "Do you want me to stop?" he asked.

"You'd better not."

He laughed again and began to stroke and fondle in earnest, until she was gasping, back bowed against him. "You feel amazing," he said, his lips against the back of her neck. Those whispered words, and his skilled touch, were her undoing. She climaxed hard, straining against him.

He held her for a long moment before he slid his hand to rest over her stomach once more. She was warm clear to her toes, but feeling a little guilty, too. She tried to reach back for him, but he stilled her hand. "Let's just stay like this," he said.

"That doesn't seem fair." She could still feel his erection, hard and insistent.

He blew out a breath. "We don't have a condom, and we don't have room in this sleeping bag to do what I'd really like to do. I can wait."

This simple statement left her momentarily speechless. The men she had been with before were not ones to wait. She was more often the one waiting on them, and sometimes left unfulfilled altogether while they snored beside her. "I'll make it worth the wait, I promise," she said, then felt embarrassed at the boast. As if she were some femme fatale.

He chuckled again, a sound she was growing to like very much. "I'm sure you will," he said. He pulled her close. "Now get some sleep."

SCOTT WOKE AS gray light was just beginning to filter through the trees. It had stopped snowing, and overnight the fire had died down. At least the campfire he had built had died down. He was still burning for Lily, who slept deeply, curled against him. He carefully lowered the zipper on his side of the sleeping bag and eased out. The cold hit him like an electric shock, but staying in there with her would have been worse torture. He pulled on clothes and began poking at the fire.

Lily groaned and rolled onto her back. “What time is it?” she asked.

“I don’t know,” he said. “Early. Stay there until I get the fire going.”

She ignored him and wriggled out of the bag, then gasped as the cold hit her. She hurriedly dressed while he tried not to watch, though his gaze kept drifting back to her slender form. “I’ll be right back,” she said, and moved off into the woods.

When she returned he had the fire blazing, and it was his turn to move into the woods to relieve himself. While he was there, he circled their camp, looking for any sign of a predator—human or animal. He found none.

“Breakfast is coffee,” she said, and nodded to the cup of snow she had set beside the fire to melt.

His stomach growled, but he nodded. “We should reach Axis Ridge in a couple of hours,” he said. “Then we can drive to the resort.”

“I would have thought someone would have come looking for us by now,” she said.

“The weather yesterday made searching difficult,” he said. “But it’s clear now. They should be able to get a helicopter up. With luck, they’ll spot us on the road. That will speed things up.”

They drank their coffee and packed their belongings. Scott was putting out the fire when she grabbed his arm. “Listen!”

He stilled, ears straining. At first he heard nothing, then thought he heard a distant bark.

Then an ear-splitting whistle almost deafened him. He looked over to see Lily, pinkie fingers hooked in the corners of her mouth. She whistled again. "Shelby!" she shouted.

A commotion to their left had them both moving in that direction. The blonde Malinois burst into the clearing and almost bowled Lily over. Hunter was right behind her and leaped into Scott's arms. He staggered back and hugged the dog tightly. Until now, he hadn't allowed himself to admit how worried he had been about the dog.

"Lily!" Jackson staggered from the woods. He was disheveled and pale, tears streaming down his cheeks.

Lily rushed to embrace him. "Oh, Jackson, I'm so glad to see you," she said. "We were so worried."

"I… I got lost," he sobbed. "I… I thought I'd never… never see you again."

Scott was already raking up coals and feeding wood onto the fire. "You're safe now," he said. "Let's get you warm, and you can tell us what happened."

He put warm rocks from the fire under the boy's feet, and Lily wrapped her sleeping bag around him. They heated water and gave him a cup of weak coffee. "You won't like the taste, but drink it," Lily said.

He drained the cup and held it out. "Can I have some more? And do you have anything to eat? I'm hungry."

Scott's own stomach rumbled again.

"I'm sorry, we don't." Lily rubbed the boy's shoulder. "But by tonight you should be home and safe and eating whatever you want."

Scott hoped she was right. Nothing had gone their way lately. "What happened after we ran from the top of the ridge?" he asked. "We looked and couldn't find you."

"I looked for you guys and couldn't find *you*!"

"Where were you?" Lily asked.

"I don't know. After Scott was shot I just ran as fast as I could." He frowned at Scott. "You were shot, weren't you?"

"I was, but fortunately for me, the bullet hit something in my pack. It knocked me over, but I was okay. But in getting away from the shooter, I lost my pack."

"What did you do when you couldn't find us?" Lily asked. "How did you spend the night?"

"Shelby and Hunter found me," he said. Both dogs looked up at the mention of their names. Scott had given them water, and they had laid on their sides in the snow, exhausted. "They both came running up and stayed with me. I was hoping they would lead me to you two, but they didn't. I wandered around looking for you and they stuck with me. Then, when it got to be too dark to look anymore, I found a hollow space at the base of a big tree and crawled into that. The dogs lay on top of me." He smiled a little. "It was kind of like sleeping under two heavy, furry blankets, but they kept me warm. And they made me feel less scared."

"Good dogs!" Lily reached out and stroked each dog in turn. "They must be really hungry, too."

"Not as hungry as I am," Jackson said. "One of them caught a squirrel, and they ate it." He wrinkled his nose. "It was gross, but I was so hungry I almost tried to get part of it."

"Good dogs," Scott echoed Lily's praise. Despite Hunter's name, he had never thought of his pet as a predator. He supposed even a tame dog still had wild instincts.

Jackson finished his second cup of coffee and handed Scott the empty cup. "Are the shooters still after us?" he asked. "Have you heard from my dad? Or the sheriff?"

"I lost the sat phone when we ran down the ridge," Lily said. "But it doesn't seem like anyone has been following us."

Scott squatted down in front of the boy, so that they were eye to eye. "I know you said you don't know who kidnapped you, but do you have any idea why you were taken?" he asked. "What is it the kidnappers want from your dad?"

"I've been thinking about that," Jackson said. "I thought about it a lot before I fell asleep last night. And I remembered Preston asked me if I had seen any people who spoke with a foreign accent at the house. He was being real weird about it. I asked did he mean French people or people from Mexico, or what? Then he asked if I had seen my dad talking to any people from China, or people who looked Chinese. I told him no, but I thought it was a weird question."

"Does your father do business with people in China?" Scott asked.

Jackson pulled the sleeping bag more tightly around him. "I don't know. Maybe. He does business all over the world. It's all high-tech stuff, but I don't know much about it. I told Preston that, and he finally left me alone."

Scott glanced at Lily. She looked as puzzled as he felt. "Preston works for your dad?" Scott asked. He thought he had the connection right.

"Yeah. He's a new hire. I don't like him."

"I don't like him either," Lily said. "And it wouldn't surprise me to find out he was involved in all of this."

"What are we going to do now?" Jackson asked.

Scott stood. "We're going to keep walking," he said. "Until we get out of these woods. We'll be near the ridge where you escaped the avalanche. From there, we can get to our vehicles." Scott unwrapped the sleeping bag from around the boy. "Come on. The sooner we get going, the sooner we'll reach help."

Scott led the way, Jackson between him and Lily, the dogs ranging on either side. The snow had stopped and the sky had cleared, but without the cloud cover, temperatures had dropped. He set a rapid pace, as much to generate warmth as to hasten the journey. After the first hour, he thought he recognized some of the terrain. The trees began to thin. Suddenly, they were standing on the edge of the forest, looking out across the expanse of broken snow. Sections of earth showed where equipment had been digging, and the terrain was strewn with shattered trees, giant boulders and slabs of snow like icebergs emerging from the ocean.

"How are we going to get over all of that?" Jackson asked.

It was going to be brutal. Scott wondered how far he could carry the boy.

"We can send the dogs ahead of us," Lily said. "They'll pick out the best path."

"We don't have to cross the whole field," Scott said. "We just have to get to the cleared area for parking. The vehicles are just beyond that."

They started toward the parking area, repeatedly falling, helping each other up. In the end, they took turns carrying Jackson. The dogs led the way, guiding them around the toughest obstacles.

By the time they reached the cleared parking area, they were sweating and winded. Several inches of fresh snow had partially filled in the parking area. "It doesn't look like anyone has been here in a few days," Lily said.

Her eyes met his, weary and sad. "They must have halted the search."

"Just as well," Scott said. "They weren't going to find anything, because Jackson is with us. Just like you said all along." He would never forget her reminding him that their job was to save people—no matter what.

"How far is it to the cars?" Jackson asked.

"Not far." Scott swung the boy onto his hip, steeling himself against the sharp pain in his back. He could do this. Only a little farther to go.

Brian's truck was still there, parked beside Lily's Subaru. But they hadn't gone far before Scott realized something was wrong. "What the—?" Lily asked, failing to finish the sentence.

All four tires of the truck were slashed, and the front windshield had been shattered. The tires on the Subaru were ruined as well, only the driver's side window broken. But someone had raised the hood. When Scott reached the car and looked inside the engine compartment, he could see the battery was missing.

"Who would do something like this?" she asked.

"Someone who doesn't want us to be able to go for help," Scott said.

She turned to him, her face pale. Then she looked around them. He could read her thoughts. Was someone watching them now?

Jackson began to cry again. "I'm never going to get home!" he wailed.

Scott passed the boy to her. She rocked Jackson in her arms and kissed the top of his head. "What are we going to do?" she asked.

He looked at the snow-covered road. It was miles to any home or business, but what choice did they have? "We'll have to keep walking," he said. "At least it will be easier terrain to cover than the woods or the avalanche field."

She set Jackson on his feet once more. "I've got a better idea," she said. "I'll ski ahead of you. You two can follow on foot with the dogs, but I'm bound to get there faster. With a little bit of luck, I can send people back to meet you."

She had already removed her pack and was unfastening her skis. She dropped them on the ground and stepped into the bindings.

"I want to go with Lily!" Jackson wailed.

Scott wanted to go with her, too, but instead he put a restraining hand on the boy's shoulder. "Lily will be a lot faster than us," he said. "She'll reach help sooner. We'll follow along at our own pace."

Lily shouldered her pack once more. "I'll send help as soon as I can," she said. Shelby danced beside her. She looked down at the dog. "You'd better keep her here," she said. "She's already worn out. I don't think running all that way would be good for her, and I'm too tired to carry her."

"Shelby, come." Scott beckoned. The dog glanced at Lily, then hurried to his side. He took hold of her harness. "Good luck," he said to Lily. If Jackson hadn't been with them, he might have kissed her.

She nodded, then turned her back to them, planted a ski pole and set out.

Chapter Seventeen

The memory of a shot ringing out, the bullet felling Scott, haunted Lily as she skied down the snowy road. Anyone could be hiding in the trees on either side of her, maybe whoever had vandalized their vehicles. She forced the thought from her mind. She didn't have any choice but to keep going. Jackson was weakening fast. She didn't know how much longer he could do without food and shelter in the cold. She concentrated on sliding one ski forward and then the other, poles planting rhythmically. The road sloped downward slightly, and she began to pick up speed, the cold air stinging her cheeks even as her muscles warmed. After so many hours of trudging along in difficult terrain, the sensation of floating across the snow untied some of the knots in her shoulders and stomach.

She didn't know how long she had been skiing or how far she had traveled when she spotted the lights of a car moving toward her. She slowed and waited, torn between darting into the woods to hide and waving her hands to flag down what could be her rescuer.

The car slammed on its brakes, skidding a little in the snow, and the driver's door popped open. "Lily! Lily, you're safe!" The familiar stocky figure of Mike Swanson emerged from the car and hurried to her. He stopped directly in front of her and pushed sunglasses to the top of his head.

"Mike!" Relief surged through her. "Oh my gosh, I'm so glad to see you."

"I'm relieved to see you, too." He hugged her tightly, then stepped back and looked over her shoulder. "Where are Jackson and Scott?"

"I left them back down the road just a little ways. We decided that since I was the only one with skis, I should go ahead to bring back help."

"Terrific." He lowered his glasses. "Let's go get them."

"Where is the sheriff?" she asked. "Did he send officers to Pandora?"

Mike frowned. "The sheriff refused to take my report about your phone call seriously. I don't know what he's doing, but he isn't looking for you and Scott. I'm not even sure he's looking for Jackson anymore."

"What do you mean he wouldn't take you seriously? You told him Jackson was with me, right? And you told Denny?"

"Denny is as frustrated as I am. We decided to give up on Howard and put together our own team to rescue you all."

"Where is Denny now?"

"He's tied up at a meeting across town."

"A business meeting?" She stared, incredulous. How could Denny even think about business when his son was missing?

"A press conference or something, I think." Mike put a hand on her shoulder. "Come on. I'll radio the team and they'll catch up with us. Take me back to Jackson and Scott."

"Now that I'm here, I can talk to the sheriff," she said. She started to move past him, but he blocked her way.

"We don't have time for that," he said. "I didn't want to

upset you before, but the truth is, Preston Smith is ahead of us. We can't let him get to Jackson before we do."

"Preston? The new employee?" A shiver ran through her at the name. The man Jackson had said had questioned him about Chinese visitors.

"He's the one behind the kidnapping," Mike said. "At least, that's what Denny and I think. The sheriff isn't listening to us about that, either."

"Why wouldn't the sheriff believe you?"

"He questioned Preston and apparently believed whatever lies Preston told him. But Denny and I are sure he's involved. He's been behaving oddly ever since we hired him. You met him, right?"

She nodded. And something about him had struck her as odd. "But if I talk to the sheriff…"

"Do you want to be responsible for Jackson's death? That's what will happen if Preston gets to him first."

His words—and the harsh tone in which they were delivered—shook her. "All right," she said. "I'll take you to them."

He nodded, then pulled out a radio and clicked a button. "I'm with Lily," he said. "We're going to pick up Jackson and Scott. Have the team meet us at the intersection of Forest Service roads 723 and 787."

A garbled voice spoke through static. Lily couldn't make out the words, but Mike seemed to understand. "Ten-four." He pocketed the radio again, and turned to Lily. "Let's go," he said.

She shed her skis, stowed them and her pack in the back seat, then slid into the passenger seat. Warmth enveloped her, and she almost moaned with happiness. Just sitting down on something soft, and in such warmth, was luxurious. She forced her eyes open, fearing if she closed them she might fall asleep before they reached Scott and Jackson.

"I'M FREEZING." JACKSON SAT on a boulder by the side of the road and hugged his arms across his chest. He was so exhausted he kept falling in the snow, and Scott could no longer carry him, so they had decided to sit down and wait. "When is Lily going to come back?"

"She'll be here as soon as she can," Scott said. "Or she'll send someone to us." Realistically he knew she hadn't been gone that long, but standing here in this desolate place, cold seeping in and hunger gnawing at him, the minutes stretched to uncomfortable lengths. Even the dogs were miserable, alternately pacing and whining.

"I'm so hungry!" Jackson groaned and doubled over.

"So am I," Scott said. "Try not to think about it."

"How can I not think about it when I'm starving?"

Scott reminded himself that Jackson was only nine. He looked around for something to distract them both. Why hadn't he at least thought to ask Lily to leave her pack, with the fire starters and mug for melting water?

Shelby sat up and growled, low in her throat. Hunter leaped to his feet. Both dogs stared toward the woods behind them. Hunter barked. Jackson sat up straight. "Someone's coming!" he shouted.

Both dogs were barking now, the hair along their backs standing at attention. A figure in black emerged from the woods. A lean man with a square jaw and Roman nose stepped into their small clearing. "Call off the dogs!" he said in a commanding voice.

"Preston!" Jackson moved to stand next to Scott. "What are you doing here?"

Scott wasn't sure Preston even heard the question over

the racket the dogs were making. "Call off those dogs!" Preston shouted.

"Hunter! Shelby! Quiet!" Scott ordered.

Both dogs glanced back at him, as if to ask if he was sure. "Quiet," he repeated. "Come. Sit."

They moved to flank him and Jackson and sat, though all their attention was still riveted on Preston.

"Who are you?" Preston addressed Scott. "What are you doing with Jackson?"

"Who are *you*?" Scott countered. Jackson had one hand on Scott's hip, and was nibbling the thumbnail on his other hand.

"I'm Preston Smith. I work for Endicott Industries. Jackson, are you okay?"

Jackson didn't answer.

Scott put his hand on the boy's shoulder. "I'm Scott Linden. I work for SkyCrest Resort. What are you doing here?"

Preston studied him. Scott stood at attention, a soldier under inspection. Whatever this Preston Smith was up to now, Scott would bet he had a military background. He had the bearing of an officer.

Preston unzipped his parka and reached inside. Jackson whimpered. "Is he going to shoot us?"

Scott reached for the pistol at his back, but the other man was faster. Preston wrenched the gun away from him, jammed an elbow at the side of Scott's head, then kicked out, knocking Scott's feet out from under him. Scott clawed at the other man's face and grabbed at his arm, and Preston drove another elbow into his ribs. Scott was flat on his back, sure he was about to be shot—at close range this time—when a woman's scream cut through the air.

The sound froze all action. Preston stood over Scott with one hand raised. Scott lay on the ground, his head turned toward the sound. Jackson was crouched, arms wrapped around his knees, small sounds of distress emanating from him. The dogs still flanked the boy, on their feet once more, but silent as they studied the tableau before them.

"What are you doing!" Lily emerged from a car that had parked in the middle of the road. A man in black followed her. She looked from Jackson to Scott to Preston.

"Special Agent Preston Shipman, with the FBI," Preston said, and pulled a gun from his jacket.

Lily started to scream again, but the sound was choked off by an arm tightened around her throat. Mike held a gun to her head. "Drop that weapon, Agent Shipman, or Lily is a dead woman."

LILY'S HEART BEAT so hard she thought it would burst. Her vision blurred, and she forced herself to breathe deeply, though doing so made her even more aware of Mike's arm crushing her windpipe. When she squirmed, trying to ease the pressure, he tightened his grip even more and pressed the barrel of the pistol—hard and ice cold—against her temple.

"Mike, what are you doing?" Jackson asked.

"Shut up, kid, or I'll shoot you instead," Mike growled.

This didn't even sound like the Mike she knew—the good-natured, easygoing friend. "Where is Denny?" she asked. "Does he know what you're doing?"

"I told you. Denny is in a meeting. With some associates of mine. As long as he cooperates, they won't hurt him. Much."

Terror shuddered through her. She looked for Scott, but he was out of her field of vision. So she focused on the man across from her, the one who said he was an FBI agent. She recognized Preston Smith, the new employee who had questioned her that night at Denny's house. "Are you really with the FBI?" she asked.

"Shut up!" Mike ordered. "Throw your gun into the woods," he directed Preston.

Preston—Agent Shipman—hurled the gun away from him. It sailed out of sight into the trees. "You can't kill all of them before I kill you," he said.

"I'm betting I can get the woman and the boy before you get off a shot at me," Mike said. "Do you really want to take that chance?"

Then they all stood there, staring at one another. Lily closed her eyes, but the images were imprinted on the inside of her eyelids, like a still from a bad movie. Whoever flinched first would be the loser—but in the end, no one would win.

Mike's grip on her throat had loosened a fraction, though the barrel of the gun still dug into her temple. He outweighed her by at least fifty pounds, and any attempt to lash out at him had a chance of making him pull the trigger—either willingly or involuntarily.

"So what are you going to do now?" Preston asked. Lily marveled at how calm he sounded. Maybe because his head wasn't the one with a gun to it.

"I'm going to take Jackson and Lily with me and leave," Mike said. "I just have to get you out of the way first."

He moved the gun away from her and pointed it at the FBI agent. Lily yelped and squirmed against him. And then she and Mike were both on the ground, Shelby on top of them, her teeth clamped down on Mike's hand as he screamed and kicked.

The three of them struggled briefly, then Preston said, "Call off your dog. I've got him now." Preston stood over them, gun in one hand, cuffs in the other.

"Shelby! No! Sit!" Lily struggled to a sitting position herself. She had to give the commands again before the dog released her hold on Mike. Preston pulled Mike to his feet and cuffed his hands behind his back.

"I'm bleeding!" Mike complained. "That dog tried to kill me."

Preston only shook his head.

"I should have known you'd have another gun," Mike said.

"The gun isn't his, it's mine." Scott moved in to help Lily up. Scott held her tightly for a long moment, neither of them speaking.

"It was close enough for me to grab," Preston said. He pocketed Scott's pistol. "Come on. We need to get out of here. We have a couple of choppers coming to meet us."

Moments later, as the five people and two dogs stepped from the woods into the clearing once more, the throb of helicopter rotors cut the air. The first had barely touched down on the snow when the door opened and Denton Endicott leaped out. "Jackson!" he shouted over the din of the helicopter.

"Dad!" Jackson raced toward his father, and Denny knelt to embrace him. Lily was relieved to see him. Had Mike lied when he said Denny was being held by his associates?

Preston turned to them. "You two and the boy can go with Endicott," he said. "I'll take Mike with me."

"What about the dogs?" Lily asked.

Preston looked down at the two dogs, who were sitting at Scott's and Lily's feet. "There isn't room for them in the helicopter," he said.

"If it wasn't for them, you might not even be here," Lily said. She crossed her arms. "The helicopter can take Jackson and his dad and Scott first and come back for me and the dogs."

"I'll wait with you." Scott put his arm around her.

"You two go with the Endicotts," Preston said. "We'll send someone for the dogs."

"I don't go without my dog," Lily said.

"Me either," Scott said. "And I'd like my gun back."

Agent Shipman glared at them, then shook his head, turned and walked away, prodding Mike along in front of him.

"Don't worry. I'll make sure they come back for you and the dogs," Denny said. "Or we could probably take Lily and Shelby and come back for Scott and Hunter."

Scott turned to Lily. "Go on," he said. "I'll be fine out here."

"No. I'm not going to leave you now."

She braced herself for a lecture on not being stubborn. Maybe he would even try to order her to leave, as her boss. She could read the impulse in his eyes. He could probably read her refusal in hers. He opened his mouth, then closed it. "Go on, Mr. Endicott," he said. "We'll wait together."

They stood back and watched the helicopters lift off, one after the other. When they were gone, silence descended like a muffling pillow. "Are you okay?" Scott asked.

"I will be." She looked up at him. "I don't think I've ever been so terrified in my life."

"Me either." He squeezed her tight against his side.

"Are you okay?" she asked. She touched a bruise forming on the side of his face.

"Agent Preston objected when I pulled a gun on him. I guess I can't blame him. He probably thought I was one of the kidnappers."

"Mike has worked for Denny for twenty-five years," she

said. “They were best friends in college! Why would he do something like this?”

“Greed? Or maybe he resented that Endicott had more than he did. Who knows.” He shook his head. “I thought Preston was the villain in this story. When he stepped out of the woods and demanded to know who I was, I was sure he was behind Jackson’s kidnapping.”

“Denny will tell me later what’s going on.” She shook her head. “It’s all so unbelievable. And Shelby!” She looked down at the dog, then bent to pat her side. “You would think she was a trained attack dog or something.”

“She was protecting you,” he said. “You’re her person. The one she loves most in the world.”

She swallowed past a sudden knot in her throat. “I am. That’s the thing about dogs, isn’t it? They love you with everything they have.” Unlike people, who were always holding back. At least she was holding back. Afraid of loving too much. Afraid of hurting too much.

She looked away from Scott, her feelings in turmoil. This ordeal had changed things between them, but what did that mean going forward? He was still her boss. Still prickly and particular, hard to read. She knew him better now, but did that mean they could be a couple?

She wanted that, she thought. She wanted to try. But what did he want?

He sighed, like someone setting down a heavy weight. “I want to go home, take a shower, eat half the refrigerator and sleep for two days,” he said.

She laughed—because he was answering the question she hadn’t asked out loud, and because the answer was so basic. Except for the bath, it was the same things their dogs probably wanted. “Yeah,” she said. “I want that, too.” Later, she would think past those basic needs. Later, she would try to ferret out the answer to the riddle people were always trying to solve—what they wanted. What was within their reach and what was impossible.

Chapter Eighteen

Lily did not sleep two days, but she did stay in bed for ten hours before Special Agent Shipman rang her doorbell until she was forced to answer it. This time he held up his identification. "We need to interview you about what happened with you and Jackson," he said.

A woman with a long, narrow dark face and carefully braided hair stepped out from behind him. "I'm Special Agent Green," she said. She held up a cardboard to-go cup. "I have coffee."

Shelby peered out from around Lily's legs and growled. Preston frowned at the dog. "That dog doesn't like me much," he said.

That makes two of us, Lily thought. "She's very protective," she said. She held the door open wider. "Don't make any sudden moves and you'll be fine." She really didn't believe Shelby would attack him unprovoked, but she enjoyed the uneasy look on his face after she said the words. "Let me get dressed, and I'll talk to you." She didn't give him time to respond, merely left the room, Shelby close after her.

By the time she had dressed, combed her hair and brushed her teeth, she was feeling more human. "Thanks for the coffee," she said to Agent Green, and sipped from the cup. It was still fairly hot, and tasted wonderful, full of cream and caramel syrup. Far superior to the weak black brew they had drunk in the woods.

"We need your statement about everything that happened, starting when you found Jackson," Preston said.

"First, tell me what's going on with Mike," she asked. "Was he behind Jackson's kidnapping?"

The two agents exchanged looks. "I can't reveal details of our case," Shipman said.

She set down the coffee and leaned toward him. "The man tried to kill me. He held a gun to my head. He kidnapped a little boy I care about very much. You can at least tell me something—or I won't tell you anything."

"We can have the court compel you to provide evidence," Shipman said.

She crossed her arms over her chest. "Go ahead. Or you could tell me what Mike was up to and I'll tell you everything right now."

"We believe Michael Swanson had made a deal with the Chinese government to sell them the details for technology Endicott Industries developed for the US military," Agent Green said. She ignored Preston's scowl. "Agent Shipman was embedded in the company to look for evidence to refute or support these suspicions."

"Did Denny Endicott know about this?" Lily asked. She held her breath, waiting for the answer. She didn't want to think her friend could be involved in such a scheme.

"We don't believe so, no," Green said. "But at some point in the past few months, he did become suspicious that someone was leaking confidential information. He tightened security. This made it impossible for Swanson to help himself to the information he needed."

"We believe the Chinese put pressure on him to deliver more information," Shipman took up the story. "At first,

Swanson arranged for a couple of guys to rough up Endicott and threaten him if he didn't hand over the information they wanted."

"That was the night I was babysitting," Lily said. "The night you came to the house and threatened me when I wouldn't let you in. What was that all about?"

Shipman scowled. "I was looking for evidence of Endicott's involvement."

"You were out of line, treating me that way."

"I was focused on doing my job," Shipman said. "It doesn't matter anyway, since you wouldn't let me in."

"We've never found evidence that Mr. Endicott was involved," Agent Green said.

"Denny said he refused to cooperate with the people who threatened him that night," Lily said.

Shipman nodded. "The threats didn't work, so the next phase was to kidnap Jackson. The idea was that Mike would volunteer to intercede with the kidnappers on Endicott's behalf. He would turn over the classified information they wanted and return with Jackson. He'd be a hero, Endicott would trust him even more, and the kidnappers would disappear back to China—until the next time Mike had secrets to sell."

"Why would Mike betray his friend that way?" Lily asked.

"He says he didn't have a choice," Green said. "That the Chinese threatened to kill him if he didn't do what they wanted."

"People like this always have an excuse," Shipman said. "They offered him a million dollars in an offshore account. That's plenty of motivation for a lot of people."

"Who was the man who actually took Jackson from the ski resort?" Lily asked.

"His name was Donald Johanson," Green said. "He was married to a Chinese national and lived in the country for twenty years before he returned to the States to do dirty work for his handlers. He took charge of the boy as a way of having more leverage over Mike. When the avalanche killed him, Mike was frantic. He ended up kidnapping Endicott himself. But without his son, Endicott would reveal nothing."

"But Denny was in the first helicopter that arrived," she said. "How did he escape?"

"The sheriff's department became suspicious when they couldn't contact Endicott and went to his plant. They found him tied up in a vacant conference room and freed him. He told them about Mike."

"Endicott thought Mike and Preston were working together," Agent Green said. Her face was expressionless, but Lily thought she detected a gleam in the agent's eye.

"We cleared that up soon enough," Preston said. "Though I wasn't there at the time. I was trying to track you down."

"Who shot at Scott at the top of the ridge?" Lily asked.

"That was another of the kidnappers," Preston said. "They were supposed to rendezvous with him once Mike handed over the information from Endicott. They planned to leave Jackson somewhere and communicate his whereabouts once they were safely out of the country."

"At least, that's according to the one man who agreed to talk to us," Agent Green said.

"Do you have everyone involved in custody now?" Lily asked.

"Not everyone." Preston's face was as expressionless as a mannequin. "We believe some of the group have left the country."

"We would appreciate it if you'd give us your statement now," Agent Green said.

"All right." She drank the last of the coffee, took a deep breath and told them everything, beginning with the day Jackson disappeared until the helicopters touched down in the valley. By the time she was done, she felt drained emotionally and physically. She wanted to crawl back under the covers and stay there.

Agent Green switched off the recorder that had sat between them. "Thank you," she said. "We may have more questions later, but that should do for now."

"Did you interview Jackson?" Lily asked. "And Scott?"

"We're going to talk to Jackson later today," Green said. "With his father and the family attorney present."

"We talked to your boyfriend," Preston said. "His story matches up with yours."

She started to tell him Scott wasn't her boyfriend, but held her tongue. She didn't know what he was, but clearly he was more to her now than a boss. And more than a friend. At least, she wanted him to be more.

"He wouldn't talk to us until we returned his gun," Green said. "And he asked about you. If you were all right."

Warmth bloomed in her chest at the words. Surely that meant he cared.

The agents left and she went back to bed, and back to sleep. She slept fitfully, and was disoriented and out of sorts when she awoke. She checked her phone and found messages from Nina and Connor, asking how she was doing. But nothing from Scott. She didn't like how much this silence from him stung, but told herself he was probably still sleeping.

By the next morning, she was feeling more like herself. She was on the calendar to work that day, so she dressed, harnessed Shelby and took the shuttle to the ski resort. Most of the rest of the crew was there, and they greeted her with hugs and pats on the back, asked how she was doing, and praised and patted Shelby. Word had spread that the dog had been a hero, and there were jokes about how she should have been a police dog.

"All right, everybody, we'd better get started."

The words were the ones Scott always used, but the person who said them was Connor. He stood while the rest of them sat or leaned against the walls of the patrol shack. "As most of you have probably heard by now, Scott turned in his resignation, effective immediately. I'm filling in as interim while corporate decides what they want to do about the job."

"What!" Lily's cry of alarm made everyone turn to look at her. "Scott resigned? When?"

Connor looked down at the clipboard in his hand. "Yesterday morning. I thought you knew."

No, she had not known. "Did he say why? Is he all right?"

"I was as surprised as you are," Connor said. "So I stopped by his place to see him. He was fine. Just said he had another opportunity he wanted to pursue. He seemed happy about it."

He had told Connor all of this, but not her. The knowledge hurt. She sat back. "Okay. Sorry I interrupted."

He read down the list of patrol assignments and tasks that needed to be seen to. She half listened, still dazed at this turn of events. When Connor stopped talking and everyone prepared to leave, she pulled on her jacket, then stood still, realizing she had no idea what she was supposed to do.

"You're with me this morning," Nina said. "We're patrolling the Glades."

Nina waited until they were on the lift before she spoke. "Real shocker about Scott, huh?"

"Yeah," Lily agreed. "He created the avy dog program. Why would he quit?"

"Did something happen while you were out there, looking for Jackson?" Nina asked. "Something to change his mind?"

So much had happened. Scott had been shot, but hadn't died. They had been cold and hungry and lost and desperate. They had shared a sleeping bag, and she had never felt closer to another person.

Was she the reason he had resigned his job and left the program he loved? That was beyond ridiculous. Maybe escaping death had made him rethink his whole life, and he had decided to move away and what—he didn't seem the type to join a monastery or decide to get a PhD in philosophy. But how well did she know him?

Not at all, it appeared. "I don't know what happened," she said.

"Connor says Scott is happy about it, whatever the reason," Nina said. "And Connor will do a good job."

They reached the patrol station at the top of Lift 7 to find a family from Chicago waiting to buy T-shirts and ask questions. Then they were called to attend a woman who had fallen and injured her knee on a difficult run.

Lily moved from one task to the next in a fog. At the end of the day she headed back to patrol headquarters at the base area, only to be hailed before she could reach the office. "Lily! Wait up!"

She turned to see Denny Endicott and Jackson walking toward her. She smiled. "It's good to see you both looking so well."

Denny hugged her tightly, holding on for just a moment. "I can't thank you enough for all you did for me and Jackson," he said.

"You don't have to thank me," she said. "I'm just so glad everything worked out. Are you both okay? Really?"

"I'm okay," Jackson said. "I ate a cheeseburger and slept for, like, a day and a half."

"I'm still dealing with the fact that the man I trusted with my life tried to take my son away from me," Denny said. "But I have Jackson, and I still have my business and my good name, and that's all that matters. And you're okay. And Scott. The two of you will always be heroes in my book."

She nodded, the mention of Scott's name a heaviness in her stomach.

"I was just talking to Doug Elam about the avalanche dog program," Denny said.

"Oh?"

"Jackson told me how Shelby and Hunter kept him warm and safe after he got separated from you and Scott, and how Shelby attacked Mike when he tried to shoot Agent Shipman. In light of that, I want to make sure the avalanche dog program here at the resort keeps going."

"Dad's giving the resort a lot of money just for the dogs," Jackson said.

"Well, and their handlers and trainers and such," Denny said.

"That's so generous of you," Lily said. *Scott would love this*, she thought. *Why hadn't he stayed to hear this?*

"It's the least I could do." Denny patted her shoulder. "You're sure you're all right now? If you need anything at all, you let me know."

"I'm fine, really."

"That's good to know. I'm glad I ran into you. We won't be needing you to stay with Jackson for a while." He looked down at his son, who grinned up at him. "We're going to take a little vacation, something we've been putting off too long."

"We're going to Disney World!" Jackson said. "We're going to ride all the rides at least twice."

Lily laughed at the boy's enthusiasm, then stooped to hug him. "You have a wonderful time, and when you get home I want to hear all about it."

After they left, she retrieved Shelby and her belongings and headed home. As she stepped off the shuttle at the entrance to her apartment complex, she glanced across the lot and saw Scott's motorcycle parked in its customary place. Before she could lose her nerve, she got out of the car and marched across the complex and up the steps to his apartment.

She leaned hard on the bell, then listened as heavy footsteps crossed to the door. After a moment, it opened. "Lily? What are you doing here?"

"I came to ask you what you think you're doing." She pushed past him. Shelby followed and hurried to greet Hunter.

Scott closed the door behind her. He was barefoot, wearing joggers cinched at the hips, and a long-sleeved T-shirt advertising a long-defunct brewery, the lettering flaking and faded. She turned to face him. "I showed up at work this morning and learned I was the only person on the team who didn't know you'd quit the program," she said. "The program you started. The program you gave everything to. The program Denny Endicott just gave a bunch of money to in order to keep us going. How could you do that?"

She was horrified when her voice broke on the last sentence, and tears spilled down her face. Why did she care so much what Scott Linden did with his life? He was betraying the program, not her.

He raked his hand through his hair. "I was going to tell you," he said. "I was just waiting."

"Waiting for what?"

"For you to, you know, recover. From your ordeal in the woods."

"I'm recovered, okay?" She glared at him. "So what the hell are you doing, Scott? Are you running away? Because of what happened between us? And what did happen, exactly? Did it mean anything to you?"

He met her gaze at last. "Did it mean anything to *you*?" he asked.

She looked away, fresh tears forming. She didn't want to be this woman, crying over a man who was leaving. But she didn't want to be a person who pretended things were all right when they weren't. "You were there," she said, her voice scarcely above a whisper. "You held me in your arms. How can you even ask that?" That moment had meant everything, not because of the intimacy—though that had been pretty special—but because of everything that came before and after. The things they had said to each other. The things they had felt for each other.

"Oh, Lily." He wrapped his arms around her, and she didn't resist. She wanted to be stronger than that. Later, she would be. Later, she would tell him everything she thought about him. But for just this moment she stood, eyes closed, feeling his strength support her, his warmth seep into her, the spice and musk scent of him enveloping her.

She waited for him to say something. Anything. But he only stood there, arms around her, chin resting on the top of her head, as if time had stopped.

She wriggled away from him. "Why did you resign from the avy dog program?" she asked.

"I'm going to work for C-RAD," he said. "Adam has

been after me for months to come work for him, and I decided it's time."

"Oh." She studied his face. "And you would rather do that than stay with the avy dog program and SkyCrest?"

"I think I can make a bigger impact with C-RAD." He looked at his feet, then up at her again. "And I want to be at a place where I'm not your boss."

She blinked, not sure she had heard him correctly. He moved closer, and stroked her cheek with the back of one hand. "I knew you were special almost from the first," he said. "But these few days alone with you…and that night…" He kissed her temple. "I knew after that night that I didn't want to lose you. Not if there was a chance…"

She turned her head and found his lips with her own. This was what she wanted—what she needed. To be this close to him. His mouth was warm and supple, sparking every nerve in her. His tongue was silken against hers, the pressure of his lips telegraphing how much he wanted her. Need surged through her, and she tugged blindly at his clothing, impatient. He picked her up, and she wrapped her legs around his waist, their lips still pressed together.

He carried her from the room, into his bedroom, and kicked the door shut behind him. When he spilled her onto the bed and collapsed beside her, she climbed onto him, tugging his shirt up, kissing her way up from his navel, tracing the contours of his abdomen and ribs, teeth scraping his erect nipples.

He pushed her away long enough for him to pull her fleece top over her head, then strip off his own T-shirt. She tossed her bra across the room, feeling reckless. Then he rolled her to her back and began making his way down her body, his lips heated and insistent. He took his time, stroking and kissing until she was wild with wanting him.

He pushed her leggings and underwear to her hips and clamped his mouth over her with such intensity she gasped. He stilled. "Did I hurt you?"

"No." She pushed his head down. "No." Somehow, that was the only word she could muster. He took the hint and returned to attending to her with the kind of attention she imagined an artist paid to his work.

By the time he rolled away from her she was gasping, and protested at his abandoning her. He smiled and kissed the tip of her nose. "I'll be right back," he said.

She closed her eyes, trying to pull herself together, but before she had recovered enough to sit up, he was back, a foil packet in hand, divested now of the rest of his clothing. She stared at him, appreciating his lean and muscular body—not the physique of a bodybuilder, but the form of a man who spent hours on skis—muscular legs and toned buttocks, broad shoulders and a trim waist.

She raised up on her elbows and watched as he rolled on the condom. Only when he reached for her again did she realize his hand was shaking. She grasped his fingers. "Are you okay?" she asked.

"More than okay," he said, and pulled her to him once more.

Their earlier desperate fervor had transformed to a quiet intensity. They moved more deliberately, exploring the contours and curves of each other's bodies, testing out positions and techniques, watching each other's faces to gauge the results of each new experiment. But as pleasurable as this was, the tension could only be borne so long. She clutched at him and whispered in his ear. "Now. Please."

His answer was a deep and lingering kiss, and then he was easing into her, grasping her hips and guiding her until they found a rhythm they both enjoyed, a rocking cadence that left her breathless and soaring. He reached between them to fondle her, and the combination of sensations had her keening with pleasure. When she dropped over the edge she may have moaned his name, and then he was moving faster, his face a mask of concentration.

His climax shuddered through them both, and she held him tightly, hands digging into the muscles of his back, his forehead pressed to her shoulder. They lay together for a long time after, until their breathing slowed and settled, and he eased away from her. He got up and went into the bathroom and returned a few moments later and lay beside her. She cradled her head on his shoulder and closed her eyes.

"I'm not an easy person to be with," he said, his voice cutting through the quiet.

She let the words and their meaning settle into her. Was this a confession? A statement of fact? Or a tentative promise for the future? "Neither am I," she said. She rested her palm against his chest, over his heart. "I'll tell you what I think without always worrying about sparing your feelings."

"I already figured that one out. I'd rather that than be left trying to read your mind."

She lifted her head enough to look at him. "I reserve the right to make you do that, too." She laughed at the flare of panic in his eyes.

"What's so funny?" he asked.

"You. Nobody's perfect. I don't expect you to be."

"I'm probably never going to be rich. The kind of work I'm drawn to isn't always the best paid."

She remembered what he had told her about his former girlfriend—and his parents—berating him for not being ambitious. "That's just one of the things I admire about you," she said. "Money's nice, but it's not the most important thing. And I know you love dogs. That's a big one."

"Yeah. I love dogs. And kids."

She stilled. "Too soon?" he asked. "No pressure or anything."

Again, she laughed. "I already knew you liked children," she said. "You're really good with them. But we'll table this discussion until later." Much later.

"Fair enough. I'm just trying to put all my cards on the table."

"Oh. And why is that?"

"I think we could build something real between us," he said. "I want to try." He covered her hand with his own. "I'm pretty sure I'm in love with you."

Her heart beat faster at the words. Frightening words. Thrilling words. Sometimes the two emotions were so close to being the same. "I love you, too," she said. She kissed his cheek. "I'm here right now, and I'm not going anywhere. That's a good start, don't you think?"

"Yeah." He cradled her against him, and she closed her eyes once more. It wasn't a dramatic declaration or an ardent proposal of marriage, but either of those things would have made her suspicious or scared her away. This was better—a tentative agreement to do their best to love each other. To see where walking this path together would lead.

Epilogue

Three months later

The sun on the snow shone so brightly Lily had to squint through the tinted lenses on her goggles. The blue sky promised a perfect day for skiing, the spring snow the texture of raw sugar, crunching beneath her feet with each step. Shelby raced ahead of her across the ski run and skidded to a stop, snow flying, at Scott's feet. He greeted her enthusiastically, and the dog wagged her tail furiously.

"Are you ready for this?" Scott asked.

"We are." Lily looked around. "It's been ages since I've been to Vail. I'm looking forward to skiing a few runs when this is over."

"Yeah, that'll be fun."

Level A certification for avalanche rescue dogs had to be conducted at a resort other than their home resort. Scott and Adam had arranged for Shelby's certification test to be conducted at Vail, though Scott had recused himself from judging, and Marcie Stevens from Wasatch Backcountry was filling in.

Adam and Marcie skied over to join them. "We need to get started so we're out of here before the lifts open," Adam said.

"Let's do it," Lily said.

"You know the drill," Adam said. "Volunteers, are you ready?"

"I'm ready." Jackson stuck up his hand.

"Me too," Denny said.

Lily grinned at them. She had asked these two if they would be the "victims" Shelby needed to find for today's test.

Nina and Brian led Denny and Jackson away. They would seal them up in the ice caves, then sweep the area to camouflage the hiding spots. Scott moved over and took Lily's hand. "Are you nervous?"

"Of course."

"Shelby is going to do great."

"Everybody ready?" Adam asked.

"Yes," a half dozen voices answered.

He clicked his stopwatch. "Now."

Lily looked into Shelby's eyes—so attentive and eager to please. "Go find," she commanded. The dog spun around and was off.

It took ten minutes for Shelby to find Denny, but five minutes later she was barking and digging out Jackson, who emerged from his hiding place laughing and waving a tug toy, which Shelby grabbed and used to pull him the rest of the way onto the snow. Boy and dog rolled on the ground while Lily's fellow ski patrollers cheered.

"Congratulations," Adam said. "Shelby has passed her Level A certification."

Scott pulled her close and kissed her. "I knew you could do it."

"That's not what you said when we first met."

"That was before I knew how stubborn you could be."

"I prefer tenacious." She looked into his eyes. "I'm not one to give up on something worth having."

"I'm thankful every day for that." He kissed her again, until those around them began whistling and hooting. They smiled at each other, not caring about the good-natured teasing. *I love you*, he said with his eyes. *Love you more*, she answered. What had started out as an experiment to see if they could make it was starting to feel like forever. A bond stronger than the things they had overcome, or the challenges they might meet in the future.

* * * * *